UnZeroed?

By John M. Cape

This is a work of fiction. Names, characters, and incidents are either the product of the author's imagination or are used fictitiously, and any resemblance to any actual persons, living or dead, is entirely coincidental. Any perceived slight of any individual is purely unintentional. Even so, the planet involved is Earth. The various materials related to the associated science, policy, energy characteristics, and historical charts are mostly derived from a collection of sources generally classified as nonfiction.

While all attempts have been made to verify the information provided in this publication, neither the author nor the publisher assumes any responsibility for errors, omissions, or contrary interpretations of the subject matter herein.

Singing Bowl Publishing, Houston, Texas
oildusk@aol.com

Library of Congress Control Number: 2024913495

© 2024 John M. Cape

ISBN 10:   0-9787893-4-2
ISBN 13: 978-0-9787893-4-3

Extract of Absolute Zero Emissions 2050

"The two big challenges we face with an all-electric future are flying and shipping. Although there are lots of new ideas about electric planes, they won't be operating at commercial scales within 30 years, so zero emissions means that for some period, we'll all stop using airplanes. Shipping is more challenging: although there are a few military ships run by nuclear reactors, we currently don't have any large electric merchant ships, but we depend strongly on shipping for imported food and goods.

In addition, obeying the law of our Climate Change Act requires that we stop doing anything that causes emissions regardless of its energy source. This requires that we stop eating beef and lamb - ruminants who release methane as they digest grass - and already many people have started to switch to more vegetarian diets. However the most difficult problem is cement: making cement releases emissions regardless of how it's powered, there are currently no alternative options available at scale, and we don't know how to install new renewables or make new energy efficient buildings without it."

Absolute Zero Energy Emissions 2050
Research Program Sponsored by the UK Government

Contents

Quotes

"The **largest threat to freedom**, democracy, the market economy, and prosperity at the end of the 20th and at the beginning of the 21st century is no longer socialism. It is, instead, the **ambitious, arrogant, unscrupulous ideology of environmentalism**."

Václav Klaus

"In climate research and modelling, we should recognize that we are dealing with a coupled non-linear chaotic system, and therefore that **long-term prediction of future climate states is not possible**."

IPCC Third Assessment Report (2001)

"Whatever the cause of the climate change madness, the effect is clear. **While global warming is not a problem, the policies intended to prevent it are a disaster**."

Nigel Lawson

"I don't blame the climate scientists for not knowing. Climate and weather is quite extraordinarily complex, and this is a very new form of science. **All I blame them for is pretending they know, when they don't**. But anyhow, what we want to focus on is what we're going to do. And I think this is a wake-up call. We need to abandon this crazy and costly policy of spending untold millions on littering the countryside with useless wind turbines and solar panels, and moving from a sensible energy policy of having cheap and reliable forms of energy to a policy of having unreliable and costly energy. Give up that – **what we want to focus on – it's very important – is making sure this country is really resilient and robust to whatever nature throws at us, whether there's a climate element or not**. Water storage, when there's drought."

Nigel Lawson

"Even if there is some problem, it is not able to affect any of the dangers, except marginally. What we want to do is to focus on dealing with the problems that there are, with climate – which there are, with drought and floods, and so on. These have happened in the past – they're not new. **And as for emissions, this country is responsible for less than 2% of global emissions.** Even if we cut our emissions to zero – which would put us back to the, sort of, pre-Industrial Revolution, and the poverty that that [inaudible] – even if we reduced and did that, it would be **outweighed by the amount of the Chinese,** China's **emissions' increase, in a single year.** So it is absolutely crazy, this policy."

Nigel Lawson

"One of the great mysteries of our time is **why so many people who are either born rich or who gain great wealth in the media are so hostile to the values of American society and Western civilization.** The most plausible explanation I have heard is that this stance enables them to enjoy their wealth with a clearer conscience as friends of the "underdogs" and enemies of 'the establishment" - even though in reality they are really friends of parasites and enemies of civilization."

Thomas Sowell

"Whoever is careless with the truth in small matters cannot be trusted with important matters."

Albert Einstein

Preface

This story picks up where **Poorly Zeroed** ends. Some material in that prequel has not been retold or summarized in this novel. This brief section is intended to give the reader some general background.

The government aggressively eliminated fossil fuels from the United States in 2029. The country went 'all in' on clean energy.

The new reality, however, was far from the government's green dream. The economy tanked, corporations fled, and transportation ground to a halt. The 'cheap' renewables turned out to be a mirage, leaving the country in a state of chaos.

Life became increasingly unpleasant, especially in the South during the heat of summer. Electricity was no longer affordable nor reliable; air conditioning was a distant memory for most citizens.

Battle of the Streets
January 2037

The bottle was raised for all to view. Not a proposed toast for a Quinceañera, wedding, or anniversary; this fluid is undrinkable. A cloth stuffed into the neck ran a half dozen inches beyond the opening. A lit torch tilted towards Marco. A soft gust of wind caught the cloth, and it reached towards the flame. He waved it off. Two strangers brandished handguns on a makeshift stage at his side.

Jose fixated on the waving fabric. Once a white tee-shirt, now a filthy gray shard – symbolic of this city's demise over the past decade. A metropolis shoved into decline. He stood in a particularly grimy part of Houston as the heavy wood smoke from countless fireplaces left a black crust on every surface. Unburnable trash piled around the lots and the potholed streets where rats and cockroaches took shelter in view of soaring office buildings that were mostly unoccupied.

"Now we liberate ourselves from this tit." Marco bellowed towards a growing crowd of shoddily dressed locals standing amidst the retreating shadows on this brisk morning. The morning light penetrated between two buildings and spotlighted him and his compadres.

An unintelligible utterance arose from the swelling mob. Raw and primal, but not something Jose could recognize.

"We should not be dependent on this welfare!" Marco yelled loud enough to overcome the murmur of those assembled. He waved his arm upwards and in the direction of the soup kitchen that reliably fed Jose's family. It was an industrial-styled one-story former warehouse not far from the Houston downtown bayou.

1

Young Jose and his two younger sisters had just left this dining hall toasty from the hot cocoa and stuffed on egg and chorizo breakfast burritos.

Many knew better than to challenge Marco, who he'd occasionally heard described as a Chihuahua among men. A diminutive figure, his bark was fierce, and his countenance determined. He rarely ate in this facility and tended only to show up when political officials paid visits. At such times, he served as an unelected representative for this part of town.

"They weaken our will to work, grow, and establish permanence in a country where we should be strong." Marco spat out. "Today, all over this city, we are ending this dependence. No more will we seek handouts to stay alive. From this point forward, we will find alternatives and freedom." As Marco continued, his tone increased in volume and intensity.

Jose's sisters pressed against him. Both were shivering from fear and the low temperatures. None of his siblings were accustomed to crowds, especially ones that vibrated with malice. Determined to pull him away, Marie, the younger of the two, tugged down hard on his hand. Della, who was almost his age, cupped her hand on his back, trying to edge him away to another street.

Jose stood resolute. He felt compelled to witness what was going to happen. He'd seen this type of incendiary device in movies depicting violent uprisings. It was a poor man's bazooka. He visualized their dining hall on fire and could not think of an adequate justification for such action. *What sort of idiot would cast off something essential without a viable alternative? Where would we eat? No one could be this stupid!* He asked Della to take Marie back to their shelter, though she could not easily

2

accept direction. His eyes pleaded with her; and perhaps their fear compelled her to take their little sister and leave.

He was surprised by their departure but relieved by it. He had anticipated that they would insist on staying. Events were moving too fast in a disturbing direction. He could flee if he was by himself but would have had to put up a fight had his only family been threatened.

Surprisingly, most people around him didn't appear worried. What Marco was menacing was too unbelievable to really fathom. For most, these soup kitchens were their only lifeline to sustenance. Jose bristled his shoulders towards another bystander. *Nobody could be this stupid. Right?*

The flame tilted again towards Marco. He waved it off again like a Matador with a bull charging in his direction. Someone in the growing cluster murmured, "Ole!" and some cheered. The mood of those present felt festive and informal. *It was just all good fun?*

Again, the firebrand angled towards Marco, who motioned toward it again as if he wanted to reach it, but the torchbearer quickly retracted it. It felt like a blindfolded reveler thrashing with a baseball bat toward a swinging piñata. Several viewers issued another "Ole" and many who had been anxiously holding their breath let it escape in a discernable collective sigh.

The next time the torch angled toward Marco, he made no effort to dodge it. He moved the bottle in its path and lit the cloth. He momentarily displayed the burning fuse above his head, and many responded with a gasp of disbelief. He hurled it towards the outside wood siding that covered the exterior. The glass shattered, leaving the wall in flame.

In short order, a second bottle struck the roof. Thick black smoke and a tar smell quickly filled the air as the asphalt shingles on the roof ignited. The two blazes grew toward each other and almost immediately engulfed the outside of the building. Several glass windows shattered from the heat while growing plumes billowed upwards from all openings, and thick smoke drifted near the ground toward a gap between buildings.

People inside rushed out, coughing, and harsh dark fumes escaped out the door with them. Breakfast had been over for about an hour, and only the cooking and cleaning staff should have been inside. Some had probably taken refuge in the warmth of their dining area.

Couldn't these liberators have done this at night when the facility was empty? Why did they have to do it at all? Jose saw smoke pouring out from similar buildings in the downtown area. *This was an attack on the entire city's transient population.* His brain started to register the frightening consequences that had just been inflicted on them.

A number of people shouted to stop the fire, but they were quickly dealt with. Marco's supporters roughly pushed these voices of dissent in the direction of the smoke that was amassing down one particular street. Several stragglers fell to the ground and, at risk of being trampled, hurried to get back up.

The arsonists admired their handiwork as the onlookers continued to watch in shock. Several gunshots were fired into the air, both from the sidewalk and also from the street, as Marco's ruffians constrained the spectators from intervening. The noise reverberated loudly, and people cowered from the sound.

Fire trucks arrived at this location much faster than Jose imagined possible, *as if on schedule.* They took their time hooking their fire hoses to a nearby fire extinguisher. They sprayed down the adjacent buildings, sending soot-darkened water into the street, and made no effort to save this one. When the walls and roof collapsed, they finally turned their long hoses and ladders on this structure.

The sound of other fire engines could be heard from all directions. Many charity kitchens had been assaulted - *perhaps all?* Police officers in riot gear showed up to encourage everyone to dissipate. They paid no attention to Marco or his henchmen. The show was over.

Despite those efforts, the mob expanded somewhat, with more people rushing to investigate. A police barrier was erected, and everyone was kept at a distance from the burning building. Jose left the area to rejoin his sisters. Events drove him to dwell on the urgency of their situation.

None of them had known their father, though their Mother had claimed it was the same man. Since neither Della nor Jose had ever met him, it seemed unlikely that he'd have shown up after many years and sired their little sister. They had never mentioned this to Marie or been able to answer her questions about parents that she could not recall.

One day, their Mother went out for something and never returned. They had never met relatives or been given family contact information, so Jose continued to hold the fort down in her absence. Had he gone to the police, a gap-toothed foster child system might have separated them and scattered them in different directions.

It hadn't been easy being on their own. Jose and his siblings had witnessed stiff dead littered around town on frigid mornings. Hypothermia was an unforgiving reminder of the lethality of cold weather, even in a typically warm city. Before the assurance of free food distribution programs, he remembered what it felt like to regularly go hungry. The furtive raids on dumpsters to locate something edible and the difficult decision of whether their putrid finds were safe to be shared. *Where were Marco and his friends at such times? How could they not recognize what their actions had just done to this neighborhood today?*

Arriving at the townhouse where they squatted, he found his sisters huddled by the fireplace in the living room. With boarded windows and no access to electricity, only the flames illuminated the room in a hazy light. A few dried branches and two-by-four studs were waiting to be burned. In a few hours, someone would need to leave the hearth and scrounge for more burnable fuel - an increasingly rare commodity in an area where so many relied on fireplaces and burn barrels to survive the season.

After all the ruckus, Jose assured his sisters that they could stay inside as long as they wanted.

He walked into the backyard and balanced himself over a small trench with a wood shelf. The water service was a utility not being paid, and the toilets in their bathrooms had long ago been clogged with unflushed excrement and piss. The stench was horrid. Numerous flies disregarded the stink and buzzed anyone who approached their feast.

Confident his sisters would stay put, Jose retraced his steps back to the scene of the earlier fire. Smoke-filled streets limited Jose's visibility, but he found his way back to the still-smoldering remains of their canteen. The police and firefighters were gone. Out of habit, Jose stood in line behind others as their regular lunch hour came and went. When Jose surrendered his place in line, he was certain there would be no free meals for the foreseeable future.

He wondered where the food customarily delivered for their meal preparation was. *It must have gone somewhere else, but where?*

Several of his friends confirmed rumors that *all* the food kitchens in downtown Houston were out of operation, having gone in search of a meal at other venues. Even several church fellowship rooms had been burned down to rid this area of free food.

Jose heard glass shattering in the direction of a supermarket. Thieves rushed out of that store with shopping carts full of stolen goods, and other hoodlums waited outside to fight them for their haul. He raced inside. Few items were left, but he grabbed a few tins of corned beef and a loaf of sourdough bread and hit the panic bar on the rear emergency exit. The alarm sounded, but no one was waiting outside that door to challenge him. He surmised that it would be a while before these plundered stores would open again.

He returned home and found his sisters sitting near the logs on the floor. He took them outside and walked them towards an alley. Away from the other residents, he opened one of the tins and shared it. They ate it ravenously and his sisters returned again to their places near the hearth. Jose returned to the bedroom where they slept and stealthily stashed his remaining food.

The other occupants of this nasty dwelling were angry. The destruction of the soup kitchens threatened everyone. Food was something you ordered from the post office if you had a street address, credit, and could afford the prices demanded. At least that's what he'd heard; no one he knew qualified.

Desperate people drove violence. Elsewhere was unknowable but this place was dangerous. Jose persuaded his sisters to abandon town the next morning; no one could think of another alternative.

They struggled to sleep as glassware and drywall were smashed around their dwelling throughout the night, evidence of the destructive forces already in motion.

Jose and his sisters escaped the angst by sleeping together under a thin blanket on the floor in their group room. The night was chilly, and they radiated heat to each other as they lay closely together.

He was the first awake as the first dim light of an overcast day found its way past the boards covering the windows and into their room. He woke up his girls. They packed up their few possessions into a reusable shopping bag.

He removed his machete from his hiding place and shouldered the strap beneath his coat. Della assisted Marie in putting on two pairs of socks and her worn-out and threadbare tennis shoes. A long walk was unavoidable.

As they left this lodging for the last time, Jose led them outside into the crisp morning. Marie wore an outgrown coat, the sleeves of which did not reach her hands. Della put on an unraveling knitted sweater that she had once liberated from a clothing donation box. Jose intended to take them north and suspected the direction was less important than the distance.

They paralleled one freeway heading away from downtown, and Jose and Della took turns carrying Marie when she seemed unable to walk any further. In the late afternoon, they found some clean water near a school and sat down and shared two pieces of bread; it took the edge off their appetite.

That evening, they wrapped themselves in their blanket and pulled a tarp over themselves in case it rained. The sky was clear, and the night frosty. Every noise triggered his anxiety and jolted him awake and ready to deal with predators.

By the third day, they reached the suburbs. Large houses, large lots, and wide roads filled their view. The exodus of people leaving the city overwhelmed the available sympathy of the locals. No doubt, the burglary rate in this area was already rising.

The following day, they knocked on some doors, trying to exchange chores for a meal and a warm place to sleep. There were no takers as residents ran them off like stray dogs. Locals displayed their firearms and long kitchen knives with sneers of resolve.

They were close enough to the outskirts of town to see miles of farmland which various residents commuted to during the growing seasons. These fields were bare.

Jose was still certain they needed to get far away from this city. Della was less sure but couldn't think of a better alternative. Distant bonfires lit the sky above the center of town at night. He wondered if these were residences or trees being incinerated.

As they continued their walk, they stumbled upon a waiting northbound train. They crossed between two stationary cars and then took special caution to remain out of sight. Following the tracks near the back of the column of rail cars, Della noticed an open door on one of them. Jose helped his sisters climb aboard. Inside the compartment, it was dark and smelled like cow manure.

Della pulled the door shut, which she believed would reduce the chill of the air as they traveled, but doing so intensified the odor. They huddled under the blanket when

Marie quipped that the stink was like where they'd been living. Della and Jose chuckled and held her tightly between them.

They remained in the dark for about an hour before they felt the strain and jerk of the train being pulled. The cars lurched back and forth as the steel connections squealed. Soon, they were in motion, and the draft blowing into the car was freezing and forceful. *Where to?*

All Opposed
January 2037

D ora sat in her office at The Lost Woods, a private
corporate-styled venue in the southern part of the
country. Surrounded by high chain-link fences topped with
concertina wire, the campus featured advanced energy
management systems and beautifully crafted buildings set
among stately live oak trees and gardens replete with statues.

Dora wore a headset in the real world and sat in a virtual
conference room in cyberspace. In the meeting room, she felt
like she was in a parallel universe; she could move and speak
naturally and engage with the other participants. On other
days, in different formats, all guests could sit on clouds or giant
mushrooms. The technology allowed many meeting options.

She stood before a mirror mounted on one conference area
wall and could see her imaged face staring back at her. Her
appearance was altered to suggest she had more wrinkles than
her actual face and her hair was grayer. She had never actually
met face-to-face with Mike. Had she only been interacting
with him, he'd have projected his hologram into her real office
or one of several classrooms; he could occasionally use a
physical Avatar, but that could get weird. However, since they
hosted guests today, this technology was the most accessible
for dealing with outsiders. This software was widely used, and
many guests knew how to utilize it.

Such meetings were the closest she ever got to her wealthy
boss. A Net Zero champion, he had saturated the country with
urgent editorials and clever documentaries. Before events
came to a head, he had immunized his portfolio from United
States country risk. Then, he relocated to a remote island in the

Caribbean. He relied upon Dora to maintain this property and other national operations. She waited patiently for the meeting to begin.

Mike joined next. His virtual body looked young and virile, and he had a full head of hair. His apparition lowered itself to the seat at the head of the conference table. He would have preferred the Mad Hatter room option if not for the formalness required for today's meeting.

Dora greeted Mike, then remembered to check the view projection out the virtual window. The scenery outside suggested they were sitting in an office high above New York City, perhaps the image that one might have gotten in the Twin Towers before their collapse. Large planes ominously circled the building out the window. She waved her index finger and switched to a freezing image from the Mount Everest base camp in the Himalayas. Dora hit another button and changed the color scheme around the conference room to match the clothes that Mike's image wore. She hit another button and altered her own outfit to match. She instantly relocated to the seat next to his slightly elevated chair.

The outgoing President, Ellen Winthrop, scheduled to leave office in a few days, opted not to enter the room through the entry door but used the Star Trek technique to materialize directly into the meeting. She had aged a lot in office over the previous four years, yet with this particular look, she seemed twenty years younger. Perhaps she and Mike used the same artist to render their electronic projections for these applications? Dora knew that Ellen had little to be pleased about.

"Is this everyone?" Mike asked Ellen as soon as she appeared. His digital representation smiled, a standard and preprogrammed expression for such meetings.

"I had invited my Chief of Staff to join us, but he's involved in a crisis management situation in a number of the largest cities in the country."

"Was that really necessary?" Mike retorted.

"You mean leveling the municipal feeding troughs?" At that moment, Ellen looked toward the exterior windows and seemed startled by the frozen scenery.

"Yes, that was done on your orders?" The sound of his voice was transmitted by headsets in the real world. Within this meeting room, it was as if his voice was being broadcast from speakers in the ceiling. It was difficult for Dora to determine which virtual image was speaking at any moment.

"Think of it as my going away gift to my replacement."

"Yes, but those dependent on federal handouts have been one of your major constituencies."

"Not this time. Those ungrateful vermin mostly voted against me this election?"

"Is that why you punished them?"

"Nah, hammering them was simply an additional benefit. These disruptions should keep my replacement busy for most of her term."

"Look, we're willing to consider funding some of your important initiatives after you leave office, but you can't be this blatant."

Dora observed Ellen's fixation on the snow-covered hills filling the windows. She switched the projected view to a tropical beach for some jewel of an island. Featuring waves that broke onto white sands with scattered palm trees under a

13

cloudless blue sky, she and Mike often used this scene for their meetings. *Perhaps it was taken where Mike lived?*

"Are you going to do anything to assuage the damage?" Mike persisted in grilling her. The power dynamics in this discussion were quite different than in prior meetings when Ellen could make decisions to commit the entire executive branch of the federal government.

"Nope, not my problem." Ellen smiled just after Dora changed the scenery. Perhaps in her mind, she had already switched to vacation mode?

"Okay, let's see how it plays out." He shook his head in disbelief. "I really want to get your insights on what you think your replacement is going to do in her first hundred days."

"Glad you asked." She fixated directly on him with an intense gaze. "She tagged me as an energy scoundrel. Without a doubt, she'll sign an executive agreement to eliminate the carbon tax on her first day in office."

"No surprise there."

"In addition..." she continued in her authoritative voice, "She'll target the restoration of airports, vehicle transportation, and the electrical grid's reliability."

"Once again, those are obvious moves." Mike's image did not convey any emotion. "She'll be reversing many of our major accomplishments over the past twelve years. What can you tell me that's useful?"

"It's important that we agree on a strategy."

"Why?"

"Just one or two years without enough food to go around and more than a hundred million people were persuaded to move into the country. A lot can be accomplished with consistent messaging."

"I wouldn't have had the stomach to pursue your 'deurbanization project' so aggressively."

"The deaths involved were unavoidable when so many were displaced. My point is that it's imperative to herd people to move in the direction you need them to go."

"They followed your lead, I'll grant you that."

"The beauty of labor-intensive farms is that it allows people to be almost completely self-sufficient. It's truly a sustainable lifestyle with few demands on the environment."

"So, you don't want things returning to the way they were before your predecessor took office?"

"No."

"You're so sure that Jenny is going to crash and burn that you don't think we ought to take action?" Mike sounded surprised by this. People who met with him generally wanted to use his money to support some project they couldn't afford without him.

"We don't need to leave any fingerprints. Jenny has the authority, yet almost no resources and we've culled most of the bureaucrats that might have been inclined to support her efforts. There's no way she'll fire up a major recovery."

"How so?"

"If she whacks carbon taxes as expected, that's just the start of her problems. There are too many gnarly federal regulations in place and other impediments that she then has to deal with. In addition, where does the government's revenue come from once she shuts down the carbon tax revenue?"

"I don't know. Other options?"

"She can print money." Ellen surmised. "God knows our team did a lot of that. That leads to more inflation and more erosion in the dollar's value. There are no easy fixes. It took us years of work to attain the delicate economic balance where we now find ourselves."

"So, in four years, you think you'll get re-elected?"

"When this President develops her four-year plan, there's no way she ever gets past the first year of it. Remember, we had the best interests of the planet at heart during my administration. Much lower energy consumption per capita is the key to our collective future."

"It never bothered you that these priorities induced a lot of misery on our citizens?" When Dora asked this, Ellen's likeness abruptly turned in her direction.

"Comfortable lives are a relic that we can no longer afford."

"Wow, that's sobering!" Mike insisted.

"Yeah, but true. Our lives used to be centered on unbridled consumption. Anyone these days indulging in large houses, oversized vehicles, or conspicuous travel must pay dearly for these excessive amenities. If other citizens don't punish them enough, the government will. We're in an age of minimalism."

"You're not alone in how you see the situation." Mike listed a number of global players that he could rely on to support her efforts if needed.

Ellen expressed her appreciation and promised she would not forget his support the next time she's President. With those final words, she vanished in a flash. No doubt she had other supporters to visit.

Mike turned to Dora. "She talks a good game, doesn't she?'

"She was on rock solid ground to continue her agenda, then lost an election she should have won. It's a little late to put the genie back in the bottle."

"Good point. Keep doing the stuff you've been doing. Use the gangs to stir things up and keep the media focused on criticizing this government and pushing environmental narratives."

When she nodded, he vanished. Left alone, she stared out the window. She switched back to the scene from Mount Everest. It seemed more appropriate.

Dora was less sure about this discussion than she had let on. In the past, her support efforts were sanctioned by the government. Mike had been instrumental in the path that the United States had taken, and in recent years, they gave considerable election funding to their preferred politicians to keep them on that path.

Now that they were all working against the government, there was considerably more criminal risk. Those involved in many different types of activity or resistance could be tried for treason, jailed, and even possibly executed. This sharp mission contrast made Dora's stomach queasy.

It was no surprise that Ellen didn't make any specific recommendations; anything she might have said in this forum was captured electronically and might later be used as evidence against her in other proceedings.

Even so, she *had* just been open about her actions related to destroying the charity kitchens. Perhaps that was common knowledge among her staff, but she had persistently and publically denied her involvement. While the footage only featured an electronic image that asserted that she was Ellen, Dora copied the entire electronic meeting footage to her personal computer; it seemed like something she ought to hang on to.

Country Living
January 2037

Jenny arranged to meet Paul and Rose at their Arkansas farm in early January. She was just a week away from her inauguration. She owed them greatly for their assistance to Eacher and Irene the previous fall. Their courage had been remarkable and led to her election.

She originally had hoped to bring them dinner, but there weren't many restaurants that would be up for the task in this area. She hoped to swing by, shake their hands, and leave them a small gift. When she called them, they insisted that they could feed her. She accepted that invitation but told them she needed to leave by ten o'clock.

She had not told anyone else in either political party that she was making this trip. She had insisted that these agents keep it a secret. It was a dangerous trip for several reasons. First, the roads were a challenge. Potholes, detours, and outlaws were just a few of the many things that could go wrong. Secondly, there was a real risk that someone might try to kidnap or assassinate her before she could take office. She might have informed her Vice President what she was up to but deliberately did not. Only Eacher, Irene, and this family knew what she was doing.

Her black limousine pulled up to their house, and the rusty chain-link fence gate was already open. The driver and a secret agent sat in the front. She was in the back seat with a female agent who exited the car first, scanned the tract with some instruments, and then gave her the "all clear" signal. That agent then put on her service jacket and some snivel gear and took a position behind the house. The other two agents guarded the entry to the compound.

Jenny knocked, and Paul and Rose rushed her inside. Their skinny teenage daughter with nice teeth, Clare, stood up as she entered. Rose escorted Jenny to her seat at the head of the table. It was a smaller cabin than anticipated, and the cast iron wood stove heated the room like a sauna. Faded, but colorful plastic flowers in vases lined a hutch.

Rose immediately served the food from the kitchen, and Clare assisted her. Not much of a spread from Jenny's vantage point. An undersized roasted chicken was accompanied by some potatoes and some winter squash. There was also some rye bread fresh from the oven. Rose beamed, obviously proud of her handiwork to put this meal together.

The sweet tea was served in glasses, and the jar was immediately returned to the back porch outside to keep it chilled. They offered Jenny some Maotai from an opened bottle, but she declined. They continued the conversation while eating.

"You guys were heroic last fall." Jenny wanted to get her praises in quickly. She had been briefed on Paul and Rose's progressive chops. If the atmosphere got too hostile, she would shorten the discussion or press a button to summon her security team.

"Eacher and Irene shared their escape story. Trapped at The Lost Woods, you drove through a chain link fence and rescued them from gunfire. One of my newly appointed guards remembered shooting at you. When we posted the video, it went viral and gave me a lot of election momentum."

"Sounds about right." Rose drawled slowly – it came out in a way that suggested that she hadn't yet persuaded herself that Jenny getting elected was good for the country.

'Please accept this small gold coin to commemorate your contributions to my success!"

"That's real gold! Thank you! You're kind to think of us." Rose readily accepted the gift, and Jenny felt relieved by her effusive acceptance.

Rose continued. "It's incredible that you found the time to come to our house now. We're far from the capital, and you must be slammed getting ready to take office."

"Yes, I've been swamped, yet I wouldn't have gotten elected without your contribution." *So far, so good.*

"Well, we were simply supporting Eacher. Our politics don't really match, but he needed our help."

"Did you suffer any injuries?"

"Yeah, the monster truck we borrowed took a beating. I wonder if we should give the owner this coin to compensate her for the damage. I'd bet she'd drop her lawsuit."

Jenny assured them, "Just send Eacher the bill, and I'll make sure it gets reimbursed,"

"Wonderful!" Rose released a deep breath as if a heavy burden had just been lifted.

"Given your politics, I suppose you didn't vote for me?" Jenny smoothed out the tablecloth while she fidgeted with the corner of the table.

"Actually, we didn't vote at all. However, we've long done our best to support the nation's programs."

"Well, when I'm President, I'll do my best to support everyone. It's still incredible to me that both parties have such different agendas. I've now won and intend to reverse most of my predecessors' initiatives from the past twelve years. It's just four years before we learn if we get to keep going or head back in the opposite direction."

"Well, Rose and I are conflicted about your doing anything that will put the planet at risk from climate change. Even so, we seemed to be heading in a particularly dark direction with the last administration."

"Oh, you don't know the half of it," Jenny commented.

"Try us." Rose offered no challenge or threat in the tone of her voice.

"The government was responsible for the destruction of a lot of wealth. However your party rationalized it, the policy results were similarly dysfunctional. A large swath of our citizens were induced into primitive farming efforts."

"Well, it certainly did decrease our nation's carbon dioxide emissions. Rose and I have a pretty sustainable environmental footprint here ourselves. We get by with very little. The only outside energy comes from wind and solar electricity generation, which we mostly use for electric scooters."

Jenny spent most of her time with her new staff and other party members. Their early approaches to the other party had not been encouraging. Yet, here she had two progressives who had found their way to the country without federal assistance or direction and were not hostile to her. She stopped thinking about this discussion as another obligation but an opportunity to explore the values and perspectives of long-term supporters of her opposition. "You know, one percent of our population used to produce all of our food in this country. The rest of the country was able to focus on other tasks."

"Look, we were fortunate that Paul's father had the foresight to acquire our ownership here. He thought living on the land would give us security and independence."

"Well, he was trying to look out for you. I'm not sure the government's actions were similarly motivated. They had to employ armies of land agents to acquire or claim vast private land resources to redistribute them to the people who now live on them. It took a phenomenal governmental effort to move the country toward our current agrarian focus."

"Yes, the previous few administrations were determined." Paul entered the conversation.

"To say the least. What have we achieved as a nation by following these directives? We essentially destroyed our economy."

"Well, in our case, we've simplified our lives with a more sustainable lifestyle," he persisted.

"I really respect the level of commitment of those willing to make personal sacrifices. However, I'm surprised that two well-educated people, like yourselves, aren't more interested in better-paying jobs or less grueling lifestyles."

"Well, you have us there." Rose smiled. "I miss my corporate job, and we've been struggling without Paul's income."

"And honestly, I enjoyed teaching," he added.

"So, if both of you prefer to do something else. Why are you content to live here and scratch out an existence under such difficult circumstances?" Jenny immediately feared that she might have offended them.

"I'm not saying that either of us is content with how everything worked out. It's taken a huge amount of back-breaking labor to get close to making ends meet. I'm just trying to point out that we've done our part."

"But, you *were* okay in a world with jobs and fully stocked supermarkets?"

"For sure," Rose said.

"Paul, you're an economist. You don't believe in the invisible hand?"

"Economics recognizes that there are externalities that capitalism overlooks. Climate issues fall in that category." Paul reverted to his classroom form.

"Well, that's an area where I'm not an expert. Our government hasn't done us any favors over the past twelve years." Jenny redirected her next question. "Clare, *you're* okay spending your life as a farmer?"

Clare was startled, though she responded, "You mean I have a choice?"

"This is a free country. We can follow our hearts."

"Then no, I'd choose something else." There was no waiver in her voice. She engaged the incoming President of the United States with confidence and determination.

"Trust your parents. I think they'll advise how you should spend your time preparing for the future."

"Clare, can you clear the table?" Rose directed sternly. "President Almond, would you like some cake or coffee?"

"I'll take a small slice of the cake and pass on the coffee."

"Got it. Just give me a minute."

Their discussion continued for a while longer after dinner. Jenny glanced at her phone and realized it was time to leave. She continued to assure them that the country and the planet would be in fine shape if they did something else for a living.

They stared blankly at her, and Jenny couldn't tell if they had agreed or even seriously considered what she had said.

She thanked them again, quickly worked through the goodbyes, and headed to the car. It was overcast and very dark.

While the outside air was brisk, her time near the stove had warmed her like a sauna and that insulated her from the chill for several minutes; as she reached the car, she realized that she hadn't yet put her jacket on.

A Secret Service Agent handed her a blanket and a pillow. She took her place in the backseat behind dark window shades. A barrier went up between the seats to shield her from any noise in the front. She laid on the backseat to get some rest.

The other two agents and the driver remained in the front. They drove her overnight on the way back to Washington DC. She was scheduled for some afternoon activities the next day and was aware she was cutting it close. She tried to sleep but struggled in the attempt. There were too many details whirling around her mind.

Since taking office, Jenny Almond had not had time to think deeply about anything. Just trying to get people on board to assume the various roles of the Executive Branch was a full-time job by itself. It would have helped had she or her party believed they could win the election.

From another vantage point, it was probably fortunate that the outgoing President never anticipated that she might lose. Had this been the case, her predecessor could have arranged for considerably more problems for her incoming administration to deal with. There was no love between these two political parties.

***

Several weeks later, the inauguration was a relatively quiet affair. Former Presidents had boasted of crowds that filled the mall. For her event, only locals and government employees showed up. Jenny Almond wasn't even sure if it had been televised. The media treated the event like a one-off freak accident that would never happen again.

The evening party was a nonalcoholic affair where they served punch and a variety of cookies. A local folk music band played some songs and the party ended early. She wanted to send an essential message to the nation: her party would not waste the people's money on unnecessary extravagance.

She had already signed the Executive Order eliminating the carbon tax earlier in the day. That action would be immediately contested in the courts, but the country couldn't afford to keep that impediment in place.

If Andrew Jackson could extend a blanket pardon to Confederate veterans after the Civil War, indeed, she had the power to pardon anyone who failed to support carbon tax enforcement from this day forward. Funny that running a democracy with full legislative support required such shenanigans.

Staying Alive
February 2037

Marco had been assured that after the food kitchens had been leveled, food would be available for him and his associates. That had happened for several weeks but stopped just after the new president was inaugurated. The city government was still in the hands of the prior president's party. Promises made just a month earlier should not have been repudiated. Yet, as more people tried to conceal their culpability with what had happened, they were.

Marco now found himself struggling to eat and had also become a target for others who blamed him for their local arson party.

Looting and burglary became the norm. The squatters even stopped postal vehicles and other delivery vans to scour them for food. He had few friends that he could count on and was constantly in fear that someone would shoot or stab him in the back.

For all he knew, there was a price on his head. He would turn a corner, and someone would shout, "There he is," and a pack of people would chase after him until they tired. It wasn't supposed to be like this. He hadn't even been paid for his efforts to burn down the community soup kitchen. They had simply appealed to his sense of importance.

He was the oldest child in a hard-working family and was proud of his family's legacy. His parents hail from Monterrey, a northern city in Mexico recognized for hard work and industry.

It was easy for Marco to cross the border into the United States. He had done it on a dare. Most Mexican citizens living in the United States had already returned to their home country, and there were no border agents that would prevent foreigners from entering. Because there were no benefits provided to those who lived in the United States, there were no barriers to becoming a citizen. There was a quick and simple process that he could follow, but still had not made up his mind to do so.

So Marco had come to Houston and then stayed. While he wanted to work, there wasn't much opportunity. His good looks and social skills made him someone politicians wanted to take pictures with. He wanted to be someone those in charge would like to lean on for assistance. He hoped his willingness to raze a local building would lead to more meaningful assignments. Now, he was among the many trying to evade involvement.

Marco was not lazy. Even when homeless, his tarp was tied down properly, and his gear neatly stowed. He insisted that he could be part of the solution. Marco reasoned that since there had never been any soup kitchens in the suburbs, those living there had access to food. He wanted to lead some raids into upscale areas not far from downtown Houston to prove his point.

He had a few loyal followers who were also being hounded. They thought of spacious houses in more affluent parts of the city like squirrels might think about acorns. None of his associates had much personal knowledge of what those communities were like.

That night, Marco, along with three other men, left the midtown area on electric scooters. He took the front position, and they trailed behind him on roads that lacked operating streetlights and were in bad condition. There was a lot of grumbling as they kept striking potholes on unlit streets.

Finally, they arrived at their destination. It was about five miles west of the center of town. These were nice-looking houses built on what had once been costly lots. They had shade trees that had not yet been cut down, and protective steel fences surrounded most of them. Most dwellings were two-story houses, but some one-story homes seemed much older and must have been part of the original development.

They passed the train tracks near Bellaire and pulled into an electrical transmission line easement to plan their next move. They stashed their scooters in the high grass and scrub bushes.

"Marco, did you have a particular house in mind?" Ricardo, one of his regular companions, was dressed in black from head to toe. Streets of houses ran perpendicular to the railroad tracks on both sides of the easement.

"Not really. I think anything occupied will suffice. I've not heard much in the news about people robbing this area."

"Got a plan?" Ricardo asked.

"I think we walk until we see one that looks interesting."

All three men nodded and followed him across the railroad tracks, through an empty lot, and onto the first street that ran parallel to them.

The neighborhood was quite different than the ones that they were accustomed to. In Marco's hood, many residents had simply abandoned their homes, and the street people had moved in to occupy them. This area felt like a gated community, though they had bypassed whatever guards and barriers were in place from the direction they had entered.

The moon was bright and still high, with only a few clouds. The visibility was good. Marco waved for everyone to huddle up. "This street is too close to the railroad tracks. I think the wealthier owners are a bit farther away."

"Maybe you're right," Ricardo said as the small group continued to walk east.

Marco found a house without a fence in the front yard. "This one?"

He directed one guy to go along the side of the house and look through the windows. As his man started moving closer, bright motion lights triggered and lit up the yard; they heard what sounded like a large dog barking inside. Marco couldn't tell if it was real or a recording. Then, a loud beeping noise went off. A police siren kicked on toward the east.

They all ran at full speed back to the railroad tracks. They dove into the easement just as two police cars arrived at the property they had investigated. As they glanced down the road where they had been, they could see a landowner outside speaking to the police officers who wore uniforms and carried what looked like shotguns. The policemen looked in their direction though they were well concealed. The officers returned to their car and drove towards them. They got out close by to investigate and seemed to be looking for footprints.

Marco and his gang lay low, hoping they would not be discovered. Security was a whole lot tighter in this area than he had anticipated. Five minutes later, the cops got back in their patrol car, turned off their flashing lights, and drove off slowly back in the direction they had come.

City Beat

February 2037

E vents had deteriorated since the free food distribution centers had been targeted in the top twenty major cities. After taking office, Jenny immediately requested that Homeland Security's Director, Pam Watson, address the situation.

After several weeks with no discernible progress, she asked Eacher, now her "jack of all trades" advisor, to monitor the situation in this agency closely. Everything indicated that someone did not want Homeland Security to succeed with this requirement.

The situations in most of those cities were dangerous and very similar. The largest municipal areas in the country were effectively shut down.

Over the last eight years, the U.S. Department of Housing and Urban Development had been responsible for relocating transients and other unemployed citizens into the country to work in agricultural jobs. These locals were not forced to move, but their willingness to participate generally coincided with numerous challenges in areas where they had been living. In recent years, the current situation would have been an ideal environment to send another wave of people out of the city and into rural employment.

On her first day in office, Jenny quietly ended that federal relocation program; there was no public announcement that might have upset the people who had already been moved or were in the process of being moved. At the time, some of her advisors pointed out that keeping it in place longer might relieve some pressure from the forces battling each other in the cities. She did not want to consider extending it for even another day. She decisively severed the transportation funding that could have perpetuated it.

When Eacher queried the local leaders in the major metropolitan areas, the local, county, and state governments needed more food resources to make up for the interrupted meals. The solution had to come from the national government, which had previously supplied those food distribution charity efforts.

Armed with a letter from Jenny, Eacher secured a door card and a special pass and used it to observe ongoing activity at the Homeland Security headquarters. At first, he would walk into ongoing meetings and simply listen to the discussion; the meetings quickly ended, and everyone would disperse. After a while, the significant deputies and Director got used to his presence and proceeded with their discussions. The meetings were long and frenzied, but nothing seemed to be getting accomplished.

Someone whispered to Eacher in an elevator that Janet Paulson, an advisor from the previous administration, was the person he ought to visit with.

Eacher met with her privately in a tiny temporary office that she currently occupied. There was nothing special about her room. There were no pictures of her family or other personal mementos exhibited that would suggest that she had been a long-term occupant. The grey steel desk and matching filing cabinets were uncluttered except for a computer screen on her desk. He suspected that her role as a consultant took her in many different directions.

Eacher described his relationship with the President. He had been primarily invisible during Jenny's political campaign but was now one of her closest advisors. He never mentioned that he had been mainly a geology teacher most of his career. Given what little information he did share about himself, he was curious if Janet would challenge his authority.

She immediately accepted him at his word and began sharing some of her insights on how the system had worked in the past. She had participated in putting the contracts with the vendors in place. In a low voice, she insisted that enough food was already contracted to restore the free food efforts. She believed they faced a significant problem arranging replacement dining facilities.

Eacher furiously wrote notes trying to keep up with her. He was hungry for detail and background.

Janet apologized, but there were no paper copies of their records. Everything was scanned and stored. In addition, her department's computer network had been wiped out about the same time the soup kitchens were razed.

Eacher had guessed that this was the situation. Still, this was the first time anyone else had articulated the problem so clearly and with this level of knowledge. He walked to her door and locked it so that no one else would interrupt their discussion. He returned to his seat and nodded for her to continue.

Janet looked at him strangely. Was she concerned that he might be a pervert? Eacher realized that he might have explained what he wanted to do. "Are you okay with the door locked?" he asked a little sheepishly.

"I'm glad you did. I suspect we also don't want this intercom activated while we're talking." Janet reached over and unplugged the speakerphone.

"Glad we worked that out. What's on your mind?" He asked.

Janet pulled out her laptop computer, plugged it into the monitor, and opened some food contract files. She seemed to have a complete set of all of them. She walked Eacher through the federal files that she had chosen to retain.

Eacher assured her that he planned to update the President on this development, but otherwise, it would remain their little secret.

Eacher requested a set of these files, and she took about twenty minutes to copy them to a flash drive, which she then handed him. He placed it in his pocket. In a bureaucracy where information is power, such generous sharing with an outsider was out of the ordinary. Eacher was sure that she was running out of options and must have feared that her termination was imminent. Eacher asked her if Pam Watson knew about these files.

Janet seemed very uneasy about the question. She finally blurted out that she didn't trust Pam or her Deputies. It made sense that Pam was behind all the subterfuge. Who else had the security clearances and system access to effectively manage the timing of what had happened?

Eacher could not disagree with her assessment but needed to give Pam the benefit of the doubt.

He asked Janet to let Pam know that she had a copy of these files.

Janet was reluctant to do so and confessed that her employment was likely ending. Such a declaration would get her axed immediately.

He also asked that she call him later this evening to discuss how the meeting went. He made a point to fiddle with his pant zipper and smile as he closed the door behind him when he left her office. It was a curious thing to do, yet he knew there was a hall camera where his exit might have been recorded on video. He also made a point to visit other people in the building so that no one ought to think they had discussed anything important.

***

Janet tried to meet with Pam most of the day, but her secretary insisted she was in other meetings. She persisted in her calls, always noting that she had something urgent and critical to share with the agency head; the secretary promised to schedule something. Around five o'clock, Pam's secretary called her to let her know that she had a few minutes.

Janet walked down several hallways to reach Pam's corner office. She walked into her reception area, where her secretary sat outside her door at an Ikea-style yellow-pine desk surrounded by matching furniture in the waiting room. Her secretary directed her towards Pam's open door.

Janet entered as Pam stood looking out a window overlooking the Potomac River. Her large office featured expensive dark hardwood and matching leather furniture and a matching conference table with comfortable-looking chairs. The walls featured pictures of Pam shaking hands with each of the past two Presidents. Janet had not been in this room before and wasn't sure whether she should take a seat or remain standing. Pam turned to face her, looking a bit bored by the intrusion.

Janet stood in front of her desk and explained quickly that she had located a copy of the contracts for the food distribution program.

Pam was hard to read. At first, she looked annoyed, but then she challenged Pam to explain why these files had not been shared sooner. She complained about being kept in the dark about this development and demanded to know who else was aware of it.

Janet assured her that she had just located them and was the only one with a copy. This was clearly a lie, but it seemed like an answer that Pam might accept. Janet patted her laptop satchel and intimated that they were all there.

Pam motioned for Janet to sit in one of the seats in front of her desk and asked to see the files.

Janet turned on her computer. Opened the directory and then showed her the various file names.

"That's amazing," Pam said. "It's quite a miracle that you located these. I had several other people trying to find them. Can you make me a copy?"

"Sure." Janet pulled out a flash drive and started to download the files. Pam looked at her impatiently. "We need to meet with my Directors before they leave. Just let it continue to copy; it will be ready when we return."

Janet was about to object, but Pam had given her instructions and expected to be obeyed.

"Sure," Janet said with some reluctance in her voice. She left her computer copying the files on the front of Pam's desk, and put her computer bag in the chair. The two of them exited her office.

Janet insisted that she lock the door, but Pam indicated that her secretary would monitor everything. Satisfied with this assurance, they headed down the hall.

Staying Alive Two
February 2037

R icardo whispered while they both lay with their faces in the dirt. "What have you gotten us into? These guys are serious."

"They've got money. There's no doubt about that." Marco said as they all stood up.

"Yeah, this is way too dangerous!"

"Yeah, but it took them a few minutes to investigate. If we hit a nearby house and leave in a hurry, we ought to be able to escape before they show up."

"I don't know. I don't have a good feeling about this." Ricardo said.

Their other two companions shared their concerns.

Marco tried to look confident, but he was pretty rattled. However, he knew that going home now with nothing to show for this trip would make him look weak and cowardly. People talked, and if that message got out, some people chasing him in his part of town might get bolder.

Marco puffed up his chest a bit in the dim light from the streetlights in the area and indicated that he wouldn't leave with nothing. His team agreed to follow his lead. He led them back to the street that overlooked the railroad tracks and chose another sizeable two-story house. There was no fence in the backyard, and it seemed easy to escape the house and head for the easement.

"Okay, this one," Marco said. "Remember, we kick the door open. Run to the kitchen. Grab the food, come back here, and leave immediately!"

They concealed their faces behind bandanas, crossed the railroad tracks together, and quickly moved to the front door of the house they'd selected. The lights inside were triggered by their approach, and a verbal warning from the video doorbell cautioned them to keep their distance. Ricardo kicked the front door open. The deadbolt ripped out a chunk of the frame, and the door flew open.

They rushed to the kitchen and opened what appeared to be the pantry. They were surprised to learn it was filled with dishes. They opened the door of the freezer, and there was frozen food. They threw what they could grab into canvas bags and ran to the front door as fast as they could. The homeowner was awake at this point and discharged a weapon upstairs; it sounded like he was outside on a balcony.

The sound was deafening and terrifying. Two of his men dropped their pillowcases full of food in the yard as they ran. Macro and Ricardo trailed them to the train tracks.

The entire neighborhood lit up. Once again, an emergency siren could be heard in the distance. Three of them dove into the high weeds and one of his men jumped on his scooter as planned. He made it about a hundred feet. A flash from the railing of the second-story balcony of the house they had just attacked was accompanied by the resounding retort of a rifle, perhaps one designed to hunt buffaloes. The bullet struck the rider in the back and lifted him completely off his scooter. He landed on the pavement and twitched a bit before just lying still.

One man was about to get up and also attempt to escape, but Marco grabbed his coat and pulled him back to the ground. "Just wait."

There was lots of activity near the house that they had attacked. Several police cars showed up, and security officers could be heard communicating on their radio from the street. Some of them went to the porch and could be heard above their heads. When they did not venture into the railroad easement to examine the body of the thief, Marco suspected that there were other porches with armed occupants. After about fifteen minutes, the police cars left.

Marco stayed on the ground another two hours. Then, the rider, who had started to leave earlier, stood up and slowly walked his scooter beside the railroad tracks and towards the south. About ten minutes later, he reached the street, flipped on his bike, and headed away with his headlights turned off.

When the shooter did not respond, Ricardo got up and followed the first rider using the same approach. He, too, did not draw a shot. Marco waited until he was on his way, and then he also left. The three of them met up back at their starting point in midtown.

Their entire plunder consisted of a few pounds of pork, some frozen potato sticks, and a box of bean burgers. They divvied it up, giving the dead man's portion to the other rider.

They avoided home assaults after that. That neighborhood, in particular, was not the soft target they had imagined. The three survivors felt lucky to be alive.

***

Marco met with local neighborhood representatives and the street people who squatted in this part of the city. The Mexican restaurant where they gathered did not serve food, but the previous owners served warm tap water in plastic cups to those sitting at tables.

"Why again did you burn down our building?" A small, thin, elderly woman with pink helmet hair glared at Marco. He sat beside Ricardo who was armed with a pistol in a holder strapped across his chest. The others in the room looked toward him like they expected an answer.

This was one of those questions that he ought to have had an answer for. He had often heard this asked when people weren't chasing him.

He had burned their soup kitchen to the ground based on directions from high-level city officials.

"The city asked me to burn one building. Remember, some firemen and policemen showed up and had no issues with what we were doing."

"Can you explain why they wanted all these facilities destroyed?" The same woman continued with considerable frustration in her voice.

"No. I never got an explanation. I understand that similar events happened all over the country."

"And you went along with this because..." she let the question sink into those in this room.

Marco was getting nervous. This was shaping up to be a bitch session about what had happened. Since the fire, he had been forced to fight his way out of similar discussions. "I was following orders that I assumed were legitimate."

The representatives in this room may or may not control what others did, but he did not want to antagonize them or those they would update. "Does anyone here have access to food that they can share?" Marco asked.

No one in the room volunteered to share, and several of them thought it funny that Marco would have the cajones to ask. Had their misfortune simply resulted from a hurricane, people would have readily supported each other, expecting the emergency to be only temporary. The current situation felt very different, more permanent.

One thing for sure is that many people left this area. It wasn't clear where they had gone, but they had access to something if they were still hanging around in this part of town. Even so, there were signs that people were getting desperate. Cats, dogs, pigeons, squirrels, doves, and crows were all edible and scarce.

"I see," he said when no one offered any assistance.

"What does the city suggest we do?" The elderly woman asked him carefully.

"The City wants the violence to stop. Too many homes are being invaded, and too many residents and invaders are dying."

"Why would anyone be surprised by the violence?" She asked. "Hasn't the city done anything constructive?"

"They have shut down the schools and are trying to divert the food for school lunches to those in need."

"Where?" Someone in the back asked.

"I think you must direct those questions to the school administrators."

"Anything else?"

"Some of the collectives on the outskirts of town are inviting people to join them. They've stored food from last growing season that should allow newcomers to survive the rest of the winter."

"How do we locate them?"

"The city is coordinating these opportunities. There's a line at City Hall where you can register."

"Anything else?"

"I've heard that some ships donate food at the ports."

"Is that real?"

"I'm not sure. It may just be a rumor."

A representative spoke up: "We just got another load of ammunition from the post office. If any other residents need restocking, please contact me directly." He gave his phone number to the group.

"Is that a threat?" Marco said as softly as he could, trying to calm down some of the street people at the meeting who were unhappy with this overture.

"You take it any way you want. We're not giving up our homes." The spokesperson added.

Ricardo removed his weapon from his holster and sat it on the table. When Marco motioned for him to put it away, he slowly moved the gun below the table. The meeting ended abruptly as the two rose and warily backed out of the building.

Down Home
February 2037

The winter had been a challenge. Except for the brief respite when Jenny Almond had visited them, it had been a difficult period.

Chillier than other years in recent memory, Paul and Rose had gotten by on their dwindling food stores. Delivered food or retail groceries were outside their budget. With neither breadwinner employed, they were single-mindedly focused on raising enough nourishment to meet their needs until next season's crops were ready to harvest.

While electricity prices soared during the most frigid spells, their wood stove and logs allowed them to deal with the wintry weather. Everyone else in their neighborhood had the same option, and the smoke outside sat like dark clouds over the whole community. At times, it limited visibility and made it difficult to breathe. The tree lines were receding away from the roads as the most accessible trees were felled and consumed.

Expensive electricity meant no television, computer time, or even equipment charging. Even wearing clean clothes was a luxury since they rarely ran the washer.

During the months when electricity was most expensive, they even chose not to charge their phones. This situation left them mostly disconnected from current events and distant friends and family.

On the other hand, March was a shoulder month; the polar vortexes in the winter and the hottest days of summer were forgotten, at least where they lived in Arkansas. Furthermore, the wind turbines burst into life in the best month for flying kites. There was also little demand for heating or cooling during this season, meaning electricity availability and affordability were as good as they would get.

That mattered little to Paul and Rose. Without savings or income, even cheaper electricity prices were still not affordable. They might have spent their gold coin, but simply holding it gave them comfort that they were not without resources.

They did their best not to dread the approach of summer, but it was never far from their thoughts. While their house had a perfectly operational air conditioning system, they could rarely afford to use it. Yet such inevitability only made their current cool and comfortable weather more precious.

Spring was a busy time of year. The fields required considerable dedication, and little farming equipment was available. The regular rains germinated their garden seeds. The occasional deluges also stoked the weeds that needed to be ripped from the ground by hand – before they choked out the other plants.

Because batteries slowly lost their charge, even if they weren't used, the scooters were only charged when they anticipated they needed them. They had not been fully charged in months.

Clare regularly attended school and caught the bus passing by their house each weekday. She also took the school bus back home – otherwise, she would have been stranded at school and a reasonable distance from home.

One afternoon, Paul watched the afternoon school bus pass by their house without stopping. He immediately feared that something had happened to Clare. He rushed to locate his phone and found a text message from a phone number he didn't recognize. She was staying after school for something and had arranged a ride home.

Relieved that Clare had the situation under control, he was still uncomfortable with her absence. There weren't many neighbors nearby who had children who went to high school. Of the ones that did, there weren't any that he was aware of that drove their kids to or from school. Almost all took the bus.

Paul and Rose were having a late dinner and waited impatiently for her return. They heard a noise outside and heard her footsteps on the wooden porch.

Paul wanted answers but didn't want to throttle her with questions. Rose had no hesitation.

"How did you get home?" Rose peppered Clare almost the instant she walked through the door. She and Paul rose from the sofa together to face her in the hall.

"I caught a ride."

"And why didn't you catch the bus?" Rose continued.

"School project. He's got a laptop computer."

"He?" Rose said with a rising intonation that revealed her primary concern.

"Yes," came her short reply. At this point, Clare immediately left the living room, tossed her backpack in a chair at the dining table, and headed to her room. She had either already eaten or was content to miss dinner.

Rose looked at Paul with a concerned look. There is no way that she would have shared such routine details with her Mother. Yet, given their difficult circumstances, it did not seem like they could afford Clare the same luxury. *Some boy was spending time with their daughter!* "Who the hell is she hanging out with?"

Paul just shrugged his shoulders. This was now Rose's territory, and it seemed best to keep his distance.

"Make sure you charge at least one of the scooters and her computer. We need to be able to pick her up if she accidentally gets stranded."

"Will do." In the coming weeks, Clare stayed late many days, and Rose couldn't count all the excuses she used. Clare seemed different. She was more absent-minded and suddenly very concerned about her looks. She even came home wearing makeup on several occasions.

Rose suspected that Clare was "fixed" on someone. Whether it was a boy or girl, she and Paul were accepting either way. The problem was that a boy at this age posed a potential threat to their daughter that a young woman suitor didn't. She was needed to work in the fields, especially on weekends. Rose desperately wanted Clare to share some details, but she wouldn't.

When Clare returned each night, long after the school bus passed their house, her ride dropped her off in the dark some distance from their front gate. She didn't want her parents to know more than they already did. Why?

Clare had developed nicely since the past fall. Except for her calloused hands, sun-darkened skin, lack of beauty products or professional hair styling, she was beautiful even in her scrawny, unenhanced condition. This primitive style of living allowed her to bloom at a young age, but no doubt the flower would not remain long.

***

A few months later, Clare wasn't feeling well. She hardly ate anything and was likely to throw up whatever she ate.

It wasn't unusual to get bitten by something when you spent as much time in the fields as they did. Rose was concerned – especially if it was something serious like a tick or spider bite. She kept watching Clare closely to see if she could ascertain what was going on.

Rose also spent time online and used artificial intelligence apps that could assist her in self-diagnosing. Rose typed in the various symptoms. She noted no redness or swelling associated with any potential bite location. She described it thoroughly and then pressed a button to trigger the diagnosis.

The first suggestion was pregnancy or some other type of hormone issue. "That's it!" Rose said aloud to herself. "She must be going through something hormonal!"

Rose flashed back to her own youth, where she remembered bouts of pimple assaults, her first menstrual cycles, and other aches and pains that her own Mother had recognized. Rose herself had often milked such symptoms to avoid family engagements that she was not enthralled with.

A few weeks later, Clare felt better, but she now seemed to be gaining weight! "Well, at least she's no longer starving herself!" Rose noted, reassured that their daughter did not have some type of eating disorder.

Clare was also regularly riding the school bus home in the evening – which allayed Rose's concerns about her potential risks from boy trouble.

City Beat Two
February 2037

Pam personally walked Janet to meet all of her top subordinates. She indicated that Janet could be of considerable assistance in their ongoing efforts. During one such exchange, Pam took a phone call and moved into the hallway. Janet exchanged her business card with each of the directors, and after making the rounds, the two of them returned to Pam's suite.

Janet's work case was missing when they entered her office, and her computer was gone. The secretary had already left for the day, and the office door was still unlocked. Pam thought her secretary must have secured it someplace, but she couldn't reach her by phone. "Don't sweat it," Pam assured her. "They'll turn up."

When Janet returned to the office she had been using, her personal laptop bag was also missing. It had been locked in a filing cabinet, but someone else must have had a key.

Later that evening, Janet called Eacher and explained what had happened. Eacher was very concerned but still wanted to give Pam the benefit of the doubt. He asked her to contact the secretary and retrieve her computer bags the following day.

Janet walked into the secretary's office the following day to get her bag back. The secretary did not know anything about the computer that had been left in Pam's office nor the one that turned up missing from Janet's room. She had an official document on her desk that immediately terminated Janet's employment. She called a security guard to escort Janet out of the building and confiscated her access card.

The security guard escorted Janet to her car, and she drove out of the complex. She called Eacher in tears and explained what had happened.

***

Eacher quickly located Jenny and updated her on these developments. She directed her chief of staff to immediately relieve Pam of her position; as a long-term federal employee, she could not be easily dismissed, but Jenny had her reassigned to a different agency where she would do less damage.

Eacher proposed that Janet take Pam's place. Jenny agreed and asked her chief of staff to handle that transition quickly.

Eacher called Janet back and gave her the good news. She asked if Janet needed to terminate any more of the agency's directors. She didn't think so, but she would send them packing herself if they couldn't get with the program.

When Janet returned to work the following day, her reception was a lot more encouraging than her exit had been the day before. Several lower-level employees stopped by to convey their congratulations, though none of the Directors had appeared.

Janet assumed the role with ease. Immediately assigning staff to implement all the existing contracts, she notified the existing Directors that they were on a short leash. She had the information technology team quickly restore the computer network from existing backup files, which were not difficult to locate.

Her team interacted with the regional heads of all the various cities. They arranged for churches, schools, and conference facilities in those local areas to prepare and serve the food.

Janet selected a number of her trusted associates to coordinate directly with the food delivery organizations and the local and regional experts. Within the following week, food was being served in many facilities. Within two weeks, all cities had at least one facility back in operation.

This development took the pressure off the ongoing conflicts in the major cities. Once the charity kitchens were operational, the homeless and resource-challenged populations shifted around the cities to adapt to the new locations, the locals stood down with their neighborhood protection efforts, and public transportation started to move again.

Another discovery for Jenny and Eacher was that the food source for these programs was a small number of commercial-scale farming operations around the country.

These contracts exempted them from most of the restrictions that had crippled a lot of other businesses – but only for the benefit of these specific contracts. These businesses had never had a problem buying fertilizer and were entitled to purchase gasoline or diesel at world prices; they also did not have to pay any carbon taxes for fuel used for their operations and distribution requirements. The contracts were tightly written, and these operations were constrained to produce only what was specified.

Eacher couldn't get over the question of how many other similar government deals had been agreed to. It was as if a shadow economy existed where companies provided the government with goods and services in exchange for regulatory exceptions that allowed them to be profitable. It was crony capitalism at its best.

He wondered if there was a way to use that toehold to improve living circumstances for millions more.

Even after many of the food centers were back in service, the media reported daily that most major cities were still in chaos. These reports conflicted with what was being reported by local officials but were amplified on the Internet. Jenny received reports from reliable sources that the soup kitchen restoration project had succeeded; a relative calmness descended over the affected downtown areas.

***

This experience convinced Jenny early in her administration that she was way over her head working with a federal bureaucracy that had been hired and promoted based on their enthusiasm for Net Zero policy and other party-specific outcomes associated with her predecessors.

Even eliminating the carbon tax here would take several years to undo all the regulatory obstructions already on the books aimed at confounding industry and energy access. Worse yet, environmental activists challenged every one of her Executive Orders in court, and the judges often delayed or blocked their implementation.

It was true that many of these federal bureaucrats were experts well-versed with what she needed reversed or replaced. Her advisors warned her that these personnel were critical to her mission. But given their questionable loyalty to her agenda, she didn't think they were worth the trouble. Would the precise rules matter if her underlings didn't have the budget, staff, or resources to enforce them?

The next day, she directed all her government departments to cut their staff by two-thirds. While this order was blatantly against the law, it was justifiable since funding was not available to support them. Many good people were let go, and she did her best to talk to a number of them as they left their offices for the last time.

The junior staff basically disappeared, and most of the senior staff assumed lower-level roles. This left bureaucrats who still supported Net Zero policies but were so short-handed that little regulatory enforcement occurred. Jenny only issued Executive Orders that didn't matter; that way, when the activists challenged them in court, they caused little damage regardless of whether her administration won or lost.

She also directed the post office to step up ammunition and gun delivery through the postal service. This would undoubtedly empower certain bad actors that might go postal. Still, it would also allow ordinary citizens to defend themselves, their families, and their homesteads. She was confident that many more Americans were trustworthy than were not. Essentially, Jenny was deputizing a vast expanse of the country.

Empowering individuals, especially when law enforcement was in short supply, seemed an unavoidable way to get this country back on track. It was admittedly a bit of a social experiment that she deemed inescapable.

These various actions earned her the nickname of Wild West Jenny. Suffice it to say that the news services had a field day with that moniker. As expected, the mainstream media rarely reported her administration's successes.

It had only been a short time since she had taken office, but already she felt like the country was not moving fast enough. If they couldn't convince the public that her changes were an improvement, she would not be re-elected, and the government would revert to the previous game plan.

Carbon Dreams
March 2037

S tephen Watson electronically posted the price of gasoline for the first time in nine years. Not far from the port, the fuel tanks at this gas station were filled to capacity. Now, with prices eighty percent lower, he was curious to see the response.

Within ten minutes, a chopper roared by his filling station at speed. It was followed by a wave of other motorcycles exiting the Interstate and driving into the fuel lanes by each pump.

Over the past century, motorized bikes were first dominated by rebellious youth. Then, partly because of the high costs involved, they became somewhat dominated by wealthy geezers riding off into the sunset of their lives, trying to recapture their youth. Clad in leather and featuring hand-painted helmets and bike art, their bikes were powerful, expensive, and covered in chrome. They cared little for the price of fuel, even in recent years.

Various gangs also went for high-powered bikes. However, the prevalence of such vehicles among their brethren suggested that they were in someone's employ. These bikes got mediocre gas mileage but were great for escape or pursuit.

A different crowd drove much smaller and less powerful cycles that could notch eighty miles a gallon. Still, none of those ordinary riders were among those refueling.

Stephen was terrified. From their appearance, he was sure this was a dangerous group of riders. For weeks, there had been reports of similar packs of riders attacking and robbing gas stations throughout the country. He half expected a rock to come through a store window at any moment.

55

The bikers wore a mix of outfits. One, whose hairy chest and long beard were matted with bugs, wore a leather vest with no helmet.

A second biker with a skull tattoo on his neck entered the merchandise area with a complex steel brace attached to his head that wired his jaw together. He walked awkwardly with a hitch and delivered a look that he needed to break something. He grabbed a can of chicken broth off the shelf, along with a straw, and presented a business credit card to pay for the group's fuel and snacks.

Stephen quickly tabulated the transaction and gave the soup guy a faint smile. One growl and he would have fled out of the back of the store. He swiped the card and gave it back to its owner, who signed the form. He sensed that today was his lucky day and that these badasses were aimed at something else.

The bikers mounted up and revved their motors in anticipation. The motorcycles established a formation together and then road off the property. The roar of their engines was so thunderous that it shook the shelves. Stephen breathed a sigh of relief as this gang headed out and away.

***

Just outside of Houston, the riders broke into smaller groups and started targeting vehicles on the road.

The first group took off after a fuel truck. This truck was moving gasoline from a port near Houston to the Fort Worth area.

Gus, the driver of the truck and the lone occupant, heard the bikes before he could see them. Ignoring them initially, they pulled up beside his vehicle and motioned for him to pull over to the shoulder; he tapped his ear as if he was hard of hearing. Then, he elected to floor the gas pedal and swing his truck toward their lane. Surprised, they braked hard, then gunned their engines to catch up.

Gus's truck traveled at nearly ninety miles an hour and started passing up other vehicles in the left lane of two northbound travel lanes. Gus laid on his horn as he approached cars or scooters in front of him. There were a few close calls where a few drivers did not move out of his way with sufficient urgency.

The motorcycles sped behind him for the better part of five miles. He would swerve toward them when they tried to pass on one side or the other. He succeeded in driving one off the highway and onto an exit road.

The riders behind elected to shoot his rear tires.

The lead biker moved close to the back of the truck with a sawed-off shotgun. He fired at the two tires on the right rear as he got close; those were shredded, but it was an eighteen-wheeler, and the set of tires in front of them was still intact. They aimed at the four tires on the left side. This time, they took out the two tires in the rear and one of the tires in front of it. This still left two rear working tires on the right side and one on the left side, which was dangerous for a fully loaded fuel truck moving at high speed.

On the Road
March 2037

Jose and his sisters had gotten off their train in Nacogdoches, a small town that none of them had ever heard of. They later learned that it was the oldest town in Texas and had a bit of a Spanish influence in its history, which encouraged them. It was not a bad destination, just not a particularly unique choice. Because of the historical railroad connection, other rail travelers from Houston landed in this vicinity regularly.

While it had once been a booming college town, the student population had shrunk considerably. It was now a regional center of the small farms that spread around it.

When they first arrived, they begged for money and food near a corner store and a restaurant. There was some sympathy for them, but less than they hoped. An elderly woman named Margarita owned a nearby farm and had somehow learned of their arrival. She found them just outside a restaurant.

She invited them to stay and work at her house. They instantly accepted, and Margarita walked them back to her home. She fed them and then spent some time explaining some farming basics. None of the three children knew anything about planting or harvesting. Margarita seemed patient and somewhat motherly but focused mainly on outlining her expectations regarding their work responsibilities.

Their primary task at this time of year was to clear the fields and plant the spring crops. There were no machines to assist with these activities, nor were there any mules or horses that could share in the workload. She allowed them to pick through a trunk full of old children's clothes and shoes, and they secured a few more items they could wear.

The next day, she woke them up at dawn and had them complete an hour of chores before she fed them breakfast. Later, as they stood in the fields and watched other children catch a school bus, their day was just getting started. Jose and Della did most of the work, but Marie was also tasked.

Margarita was very kind in showing them how to use the tools that she had available, which seeds to plant in which area, and how to haul water buckets from her water pump to the field. It was back-breaking work, and they were somewhat underdressed for the weather.

Margarita would wear a wide-brimmed hat to visit them in the field and provide drinks once or twice a day and some food at lunchtime, but she would only stay for a short time. She'd return to the house and fan herself in the shade of the back porch while she napped or observed them working. Sitting in her rocking chair for many hours, it was hard to tell the difference. At night, she would cook fresh or stored vegetables for their dinner. Their efforts kept them busy and earned them food and shelter. It seemed a fair deal.

They could have lasted a long time with her. However, a few months later, her son showed up without notice.

Manuel was a large, burly man whose life revolved around his ability to secure liquor. He had grown up on this homestead and had moved away at the first opportunity. According to his mother, he had been gone a few years, and she had little expectation that he would stay for long. At least that was her excuse for not assigning him any chores.

While his mother sat on the back porch sipping tea, Manuel drank whatever he could get his hands on. When Jose and his sisters finished their tasks, he was passed out somewhere.

No one woke him for dinner, and he frequently woke up in the middle of the night and loudly demanded to be fed.

Manuel took an interest in Della and flattered her, seriously worrying Jose. He was the kind of scoundrel that Della did not need in her life. Della seemed to crave the attention and did not understand his concern.

One late evening, after Manuel had finished off the leftovers and too much alcohol, he entered the barn. Surprisingly, he did not make much noise when he entered.

Jose and his sisters slept in the same general area in the barn. He was awakened by Della's screams as Manuel's rough hands actively explored parts of her body under her clothing. Jose grabbed a piece of steel rebar and demanded that Manuel leave the barn.

Manuel laughed at Jose. "Little man," he said. "Who do you think you're talking to?"

"Get your hands off my sister," Jose responded courageously but perhaps foolishly to the larger man.

"You, and what army are going to stop me?"

"Manuel, you're drunk. Get out of here before I hurt you." Jose demanded loudly.

Manuel did not take him seriously, and he held Della's arm with one hand and ripped her top off with the other like he was unhusking a tamale. She had no bra on and tried to hold her arms in front of her chest to conceal her budding breasts.

Jose was not unfamiliar with violence. He had been compelled to face unfriendly intruders in the past, and while he gave up a lot of size to Manuel, he was sober and stronger than he looked.

Jose took a swing with the rod, slamming Manuel on the side. The sound resonated as if he had made contact with a slab of beef and Manual slumped in pain. While it left a mark, Manuel immediately regained his balance. When he threw down what was left of Della's shirt, she quickly grabbed it and left the room. Manuel grabbed a wooden two-by-four off the ground and measured off against Jose, who held his steel at the ready.

Manuel swung the post at Jose and knocked his rod out of his hands. He then rushed him, and his heavy mass caught Jose by surprise, knocking him to the ground. Manual had obviously been in his share of bar fights. He straddled Jose's chest and began pounding the younger man's head with his fist and open hand, leaving welts on his face and blood splatters on the floor.

Jose tried to defend himself, but he could not budge the dead weight sitting on his chest.

Della came in behind Manuel and clocked him with the backside of a shovel. It hurt, and he bent over to feel the knot where she had whacked him. She hit him a second time on the head, this time much harder with her shovel. He fell on his side and stayed on the ground without moving. Jose was slow to move. He faced upwards with his eyes closed and took deep breaths.

Della and Marie embraced him on the ground. She asked Jose if he'd be able to get up but did not get a clear answer. They helped him to his feet, and he stood unsteadily. Nothing seemed broken, but his face was a bloody mess, and one eye was swollen shut. Della returned him to the ground and packed their gear.

She helped him to his feet once again. He swayed back and forth and then collapsed to the floor. She got a pitcher of cold water and poured it on his head. He sputtered but seemed to gain some awareness.

Della and Marie raised him to a standing position again, and then he leaned on Della as she led him out the door. When they got outside, they slowly returned to the rail yard. They found another open sidecar, and Della assisted Jose and Marie as they climbed aboard. Several hours later, the train was moving

Carbon Dreams Two
March 2037

G us called for help on his CB radio, and another truck just ahead answered. They agreed to slow down together and force the riders to stay behind them. It worked for the moment. The motorcycles were forced to follow.

So far, Gus was not particularly worried. He'd encountered similar pirates in the past and had always been able to deal with them. Even so, he was driving what was essentially a high-speed bomb. One miscalculated veer and the resulting explosion would kill anyone in the immediate area and leave a massive crater in the road.

One crazy thug took an exit ramp, sped up a lane to a stop sign, and blew through it. He barely missed a vehicle on the overpass and raced down the freeway access lane unscathed. He succeeded in getting in front of the two trucks.

The two truck drivers watched him pull off this stunt, and Gus looked at the driver in the next lane with concern. This nut was determined.

That biker in front of them moved his bike to the middle of the two lanes, pulling a box of nails out of his leather jacket. He scattered four-inch nails in each of the two lanes behind him. Punctured tires exploded under the trucks, and tire retreads scattered over the highway. Yet the two trucks continued. One of the motorcycles following behind the two trucks also took a nail in its front tire, which drove it off the road.

A state patrol car with two police officers entered the highway behind the trucks and turned on its lights and siren. The noise added to the excitement, but the attack continued.

Gus hoped that the police vehicle would end this standoff. It was rare these days for police officers to inject themselves into such dangerous maneuvers. He caught the attention of the police officer behind him and made a fist motion to show his support for their courage.

The bikes were hesitant to give up their quarry and continued to follow. The police car came up behind them and used a loudspeaker to command them to pull over and desist from their pursuit.

Out came the sawed-off shotgun, and a blast at the front of the police cruiser took out its left front tire and the radiator. The state police car immediately slowed down and pulled off to the shoulder of the road. The motorcycle in the front got word of what had happened and twisted in his seat to clinch his fist at the two trucks behind him. Gus made no expression in response.

A larger group of motorcycles caught up with them about ten miles later. One biker was holding dynamite and waving it at the truck. At Gus's insistence, the truck to his right slowed down, and all the bikers focused on Gus's rig – leaving the other transport alone for the time being. Gus picked up speed again, and the motorcycles followed. The frame shook as the flat tires threw off rubber.

About five miles later, Gus pulled over to the right shoulder when the other truck was no longer visible on the road. He realized that he had little chance of evading all of these attackers – especially given the explosives.

Gus sat in his cab for a few more minutes and was surrounded. When he opened the door to exit the truck, he barely saw the butt of a pistol before it knocked him silly.

When he woke many hours later in a field not from the road, his head was pounding, and blood was still oozing from his head wound. It was dark, and there was no sign of the fuel truck.

A Call for Help
April 2037

Eacher's phone rang. He didn't want to answer it after a long day at the office. Even so, it might be the President or Irene, so he glanced at the display screen – an unknown caller. Now, he really didn't want to answer it. Against his better judgment, he accepted the call.

"Hello?" Eacher responded, determined not to give the caller any information to continue the discussion – especially if it was a solicitor.

"Eachy, so good to hear your voice!"

Eacher paused. He recognized that voice, and that nickname was unmistakable. "Jasmine? What a surprise!" *Actually, it was more of a shock!* This woman he had lived with for almost twenty years was technically still married to him. He hadn't heard from her in a decade and a half. It immediately occurred to him that she would only call if she needed something. "How are you doing?" He asked more out of curiosity than concern.

"I think it's time that we end our separation." She stated flatly and with no attempt at small talk.

Now, he was stunned. He had made a good-faith effort to tie up the loose ends of their break, but she had never previously cooperated. He was in no hurry but had tried to resolve this very concern. "Ah, finally, time to finalize our divorce paperwork?"

"That's not what I meant." She said with some indignation. "You know, when we married, we both took vows that we'd stay together as long as we lived. I'm ready to continue my promises."

69

Eacher was unsure he'd heard correctly, but his response was more startled than welcoming. "You what?"

"I want to come home," she said.

"Where are you?" He asked weakly. He had been the one who had been heartbroken when she left. He'd always forgiven her for her exit. His career choices had driven her off. Being a climate skeptic was like wearing a "kick me" sign on his butt; it was no surprise that his tenure track evaporated. Eacher never blamed her for her decision to leave or even felt that she had acted unreasonably.

Signing the official papers would have taken a particular consideration, which had been missing during their last few years together. Just before they split, they were always fighting about something.

Eacher had no expectations of ever getting married again. If she could live in an undefined relationship state, he could too. He stopped concerning himself with the paperwork that would make their split official. So what? Many such details were bypassed in the challenged world where they both struggled to make ends meet. Any contractual force that their marriage might still have had never entered his mind as a concern before.

This declaration that she wanted to return to their marriage was a complete surprise. *What about Irene?*

"I'm in Louisiana, and things are getting a little uncomfortable here," she stated flatly. "It's my understanding that you've moved to Washington DC."

"How did you hear that?"

"I saw you on TV a few months ago. They were interviewing you while you were working on President Almond's campaign. Boy, did you bet on the right horse!"

"Is this a good number for you?" Eacher asked. "I need to do something."

"Not really, my phone battery is almost dead." She gave him the number of a woman in her church where he could leave a message.

"It's okay to text her?" He asked.

"It depends on when you send it. It might take a little time before my friend runs me down. What do you have in mind?"

"Let me check something out, and I'll get back to you."

"I knew I could count on you!" She said. "You were always a gentleman and the love of my life. How silly it was for us to have gone our separate ways."

"Bye," Eacher said and abruptly ended the call. When everything disintegrated between them, he cut his losses and moved on. The loss of his faculty position was further compounded by the almost immediate loss of his wife, and it put him into a depression that took years to overcome. He had no idea about anything that had happened to her since their breakup.

Now what? Why would he want this woman back in his life in any capacity? What would Irene say if he told her that he and Jasmine were still technically married? Even bringing up the issue with Irene would likely end badly. Of course, if he had to choose between the two women, he'd select Irene, but there was no formal commitment between them.

Eacher was almost certain that Jasmine was penniless. That was a no-brainer. Most people were. Now that he had a paid position, might she and a lawyer be able to argue for a portion of his current earnings?

One of the reasons he liked hanging out with Irene was the notion that they'd stay together until either one of them checked out. She was intelligent, stylish, and normally calm. However, here in Washington DC, there was no shortage of eligible bachelors. Would she consider better dealing him for another man if this situation with Jasmine started to complicate their lives?

He had just as soon never seen Jasmine again, but if Irene were to leave him, would it make sense to have her around? The possibility of dying alone was a scary proposition. He had been surprised to get this call, and had not fully processed the emotions or feelings that were bubbling up into his consciousness.

When he hung up with Jasmine, he thought he'd immediately find Irene and explain the situation. Now, off the call, that seemed like a bad idea. A still-married man dating a different woman would not appear to be on solid ground when it came time to divvy assets, not that either of them had much. The questions were more immediate. *Would his current finances survive Jasmine's demands? Would his relationship with Irene withstand this imposition? Wouldn't it make sense to keep this development secret from Irene until the dust settled?*

He could assist her and keep her at a distance. She had once agreed to marry him, and he still had a positive recollection or two from that relationship, though frankly, his memory wasn't what it used to be. *Whose was at this age?*

Convinced for the moment, he pulled his phone out of his pocket and tried to call her back. She didn't answer. He called the other number. The woman who answered it indicated that she was just outside her kitchen window. Eacher waited as she went outside to hand her the phone.

"Yes? My love?" she said sweetly.

Eacher instinctively cringed from the deliberately inviting tone of her voice but continued unmoved. "Jasmine, I apologize. I didn't really get a chance to better understand your situation. How are you set for money?"

"Kind of you to ask," she said in a slow southern drawl. "I've had to borrow so much around here, I'm not sure I'll ever be able to pay all that money back."

"How much do you need right now?"

"What would really be nice is if you swung by, picked me up, and brought me back to the capital with you. You know, give us a chance to get to know each other again. Keep each other warm on the trip."

"I'm sorry, I'm on a tight schedule right now. Is there some amount of money that would allow you to get by for now?" Eacher immediately regretted saying that, but detected that she was effusive about such a possibility.

"You'd be willing to send some money *my* way?"

"Jasmine, what do you need?" Eacher said flatly.

"Okay, could you spare $50,000? Money doesn't go as far as it used to, but I think that would hold me over and allow me to pay back what I owe."

"That's a lot of money. Do you have an email or phone number that I can use to wire you what I can spare?"

"That's so much more than I deserve. Just use the phone number I called you on to send the money into my account," she said, somewhat relieved. Then she ventured another question: "Who will be watching your house while you're out of state?"

"I was planning on leaving it empty."

"That sounds like you're asking for trouble," she said.

"My neighbor is leasing my lands while I'm gone. He's keeping an eye on it."

"Well, we used to live together at your place, at least for a while; I'm sure I still have a key somewhere. Let me head over there and keep it occupied while you're gone. That's the least I could do."

Eacher didn't believe that he could stop her at this point. Yet, it was true that keeping his house occupied would discourage squatters. Her living in Arkansas also meant that he wouldn't need to concern Irene yet until he sorted this out.

"Okay, I've left the key with my neighbor, William, if you can't find yours. He owns the farmhouse just east of mine. Have him call me if he has any questions about giving you access."

"Eachy, you're such a dear!"

"Just let me know when you arrive," Eacher said to her as he ended the call. This wasn't over; he knew it wasn't the last time he'd hear from her. Just like that, she was back in his life. *Maybe these efforts will keep her a long way away.*

A Lucky Break
May 2037

Jenny tasked Eacher and Irene with following up on a tip from some locals that various mothballed power plants were being targeted. She wanted them to connect with the group that had sent the message. She was still wary of the energy agency bureaucrats and wanted someone she could trust to follow up on this threat.

In theory, efforts had been made when these particular plants were closed so that they could be returned to service with a minor investment and within a reasonable amount of time.

Putting these plants back into operation was imperative to allow the country to transition more quickly toward reliable and affordable electricity. If they were rendered unusable or destroyed, restoring the electrical grid to a functional level would take much longer and require much more money.

There were also nuclear fission power plants that had suspended production. In theory, they were considered mothballed, too, but those would take a much more extensive assessment. The pressing question was whether any of these facilities could be returned to service quickly after not being operated for eight to twelve years?

The concerned phone call had come from Morgantown, Maryland, where a 1,500-megawatt electrical generation plant had been shuttered. Located on the Potomac River to the south of the capitol, this plant had once supported a broad region. It had stopped using coal before the country's carbon taxes were imposed but did utilize natural gas for a short time before it was closed. It had been out of service for at least the last ten years.

Irene and Eacher secured a government jeep and power engineer to accompany them. Irene drove and took Highway 301 south of Waldorf and proceeded to the Potomac River near the unincorporated town of Newburgh. Close to the small village of Hard Corner, they followed paved roads to the plant.

The entrance was unobstructed when they arrived at the facility since the front gate had been tossed to the side. From the initial look, hostile parties were undertaking their own evaluations of these retired power facilities. That would explain the fresh motorcycle tracks in the weeds inside the entrance. Since the gates had been compromised, and the facility seemed relatively intact, he guessed that those parties could return at any moment.

The plant abutted the river by design, which allowed coal or wood to be transported over the water and supported the cooling ponds. It was a large facility; the fenced-in area was about a square mile. Two large smoke stacks, demarked in thick red and white stripes for their upper length, stood beside a series of large square buildings where the power generation occurred.

Another slightly shorter but thicker smokestack stood next to another generation facility. Long, wide ramps led to the boilers that generated the steam that drove the turbines. Alternately, buried pipelines rose from the ground, which could also heat the boilers with natural gas.

Eacher didn't know what he was looking at, but the engineer they brought described the specific details.

They called the contact number they had been given, and a man named Bob answered the phone. He promised to meet them at the front gate in half an hour.

Bob arrived shortly from the roads just outside of the complex. He was a large, thin man who seemed too large for the electric scooter he was driving. Based on his mostly bald head and wrinkled face, Eacher guessed he was at least sixty years old. An M-16 rifle was in a long holster on the back of his scooter. He was dressed in ragged jeans and a long-sleeved shirt patched with iron-on patches. He walked gingerly and was somewhat stooped over.

Bob introduced himself. He had once been a union boss here until the facility closed. Though the nation had given up on this facility, the laid-off workers were convinced that their country needed this plant to be back in operation.

They took it upon themselves to keep an eye on it and prevent it from being vandalized. This took no small amount of time, but they were confident that the nation would one day put Morgantown back in business.

They were huge fans of President Almond and thought the order to turn the plant back on would happen any day. They had recently been able to acquire ammunition for their weapons from the post office and thought that they now had a decent chance of defending themselves.

A week ago, the motorcycles showed up, cast the gate aside, and tore up the grounds all over the facility. Bob's crew assembled their militia and were prepared to defend the idle power plant. Fortunately, the bikes were gone before they mustered.

Bob gave them a tour. From inside the business part of the building, it was a cavernous structure. With lots of concrete and shining instrumentation, numerous complex systems ensured that they could safely provide significant levels of electricity. Power lines leading into the compound could provide electricity when the plant was shut down.

From high in the building, they could survey the bridge across the river and see some distance into Virginia. Throughout the area, there were numerous small plots of land and individuals working in the fields.

In Bob's assessment, this plant could be put back into operation within six months – if no further harm occurred. His eyes were bright with confidence and pride from the efforts of those he'd served with on this site.

Bob was aware of another mothballed facility in another state that had recently been set on fire. That building was never going to operate again. Those who had sworn to protect that one were ready to relocate to this facility. The manpower to manage this power plant could be gathered quickly.

They spoke about the resources that Bob's team needed to defend this site. He asked for further security, some serious weapons, and more ammunition. They were willing to put their lives on the line to protect this asset but did not have the money to pay any more than they already had. Eacher and Irene promised to relay his requests. Bob also assured them that his group could get the front gate reattached to the fence and secured with chains.

With lots of information, Eacher and Irene left the compound and headed home. Within ten miles, they were passed by thirty motorcycles moving toward the plant. Some of the bikes pulled trailers with tarps covering their load. One cover had become unfastened and revealed wooden boxes with TNT stenciled markings and some assault weapons.

Eacher called Bob immediately, who was appreciative of the warning but pretty intimidated by the size of the force and weapons arrayed against them.

A Long Way from Home
May 2037

Jose and his sisters rode their train north. When it stopped near a railyard in Texarkana, they carefully climbed down. They found themselves in another rural area.

After wandering for a while, they stopped by a pharmacy. The clerk was curious where they had come from, so they told their story. He called an elderly woman who was willing to take them on as working helpers. She put them to work, fed them, and let them sleep in her barn. The temperatures were cool in the morning but much warmer later in the day.

When that woman's husband showed up two months later, he took a special interest in Della. Jose and his sisters quickly determined that they didn't want to stay any longer and, within a few days, took off.

They snuck onto another train near where they had gotten off the last one. There were no open boxcars this time, and they climbed up on top of a railcar. People were riding other cars that were visible from their position. Jose held onto Marie to ensure she didn't fall off as the sun baked them.

They rode along a mostly northwest route into Arkansas and then climbed off when the train paused. They walked toward a small town visible from the train and noticed a junkyard on the way. The possibility of sleeping in an abandoned car seemed like it might provide some protection from the mosquitos that had been chewing on them for the last few hours. They entered the property and then heard noises from a garage. They approached someone who looked like he might own the place.

81

"Howdy, young man." The elderly gentleman dressed in greasy coveralls greeted him. "I'm Dusty. What brings you to these parts?"

"Would you mind if we slept in one of your junk cars this evening?" Jose asked while his two sisters looked on.

"Just tonight?" Dusty asked. "Where are you heading?"

"Some place to live," Jose said.

"You got money?" Dusty asked.

"No, but we're willing to work," Jose said as Della nodded emphatically. Marie looked on with a vulnerable look that had been honed from practice; she was disarmingly cute.

"I'm about to pull this truck out of the garage. I'll buy you dinner if you can clean up this mess." Dusty said.

They agreed. As soon as the car backed out, they grabbed the brooms, a dustpan, and a mop and cleaned up the floor. They picked up all the discarded parts scattered around the shop floor and stacked them where directed. Within the next hour, they had the garage somewhat cleaned up. To have done it correctly would have required a pressure washer. The grease and dirt were practically caked on the floor and the walls.

He escorted them to Renfro's restaurant a few blocks away. He treated them to a dinner of grits and eggs – about the only thing this particular establishment sold. They were hungry and polished off all the food, including all the jelly and crackers on the table. When they started reaching for condiments on an adjacent table, Dusty stopped them, paid the bill, and they left together, walking back to his salvage yard.

On the way back, they told him about their recent farming experience. Jose boasted of all the work they had been able to contribute in exchange for meals and lodging. He assured him they would be useful additions to any local farm that would take them.

Della told of the first attack they had survived and their fear of a second one.

Dusty called Paul and Rose. He thanked them for the funds to repair the truck they had returned with bullet holes. The bullet holes had taken a fair amount of fiberglass and paint, and there had been some broken glass. The truck seemed as good as new, and the owner was no longer suing them.

They thanked him again for his assistance and credited President Almond who had funded the repairs.

Dusty then explained the situation with the kids he had just met. He related their story and some of their adventures. Rose and Paul immediately agreed to take these kids off his hands, at least for now. Dusty dropped them off at their farmstead in one of the gasoline vehicles that he had just converted to run on natural gas.

When Rusty left, Rose and Paul offered the children dinner, and they accepted. They never mentioned that Dusty had fed them just an hour earlier.

Rose settled them into the guest room. They all insisted on sleeping in the same room. Jose took one twin bed, and Della and Marie slept together in the other one. They went to bed early.

Clare came home about an hour later and was surprised to learn they now had three boarders. She seemed to relish the idea of being the elder sister. However, she had admittedly lived a sheltered life compared to these youngsters.

***

The next day, the three kids were put to work around the spread. Jose and Della were tasked with various assignments, and Marie tagged along and helped where she could. Paul and Rose learned that none of them had been attending school for some time.

Resources were tight, but there really was a lot of work that needed to be done. Rose insisted that these kids could pay their own way with their efforts; if they couldn't, she'd run them off. Even so, she felt strongly that they ought to be getting an education. There were just a few months until summer vacation, and they needed to use it to learn what they could.

The next day, these three scruffily dressed kids and Clare caught the school bus, and Rose followed on a scooter.

Rose enrolled them at the school and then headed to the thrift store. She located the clothes section and bought them a few outfits each. She honed in on the shoe racks and purchased a few pairs each.

Rose enjoyed having more people around. Farming was inefficient without machines or engines. More labor was needed to get things done, and their efforts' fruits could be shared. She didn't know how long they would be interested in staying, but barring any surprises, they had a home.

Paul needed more clarification about their ability to feed their new charges. His mobility was increasingly limited. He limped more and performed his chores more slowly. He tried to help in the fields, but his thumbs and hip often ached from arthritis.

Rose was determined to make the new arrangement work.

Clare sounded less sure and described a recent conversation. "Mom, can you believe Della asked me if I was pregnant? Isn't that a laugh?"

"Are you?" Rose asked soberly. "I was about to bring that question up myself."

Clare slumped to her knees. "You too? Is that really possible?"

"Is it?"

Clare stared back in shock. She thought long and hard about what she had been doing on occasion. "Maybe," she whispered in a barely audible voice.

"It either is, or it isn't," Rose said.

"It hardly seems possible," Clare said.

"Tell you what, I'm driving to the store to buy a home pregnancy test," Rose pulled Clare close and hugged her tightly. She shuddered to think that her teenage daughter might have gotten knocked up but was no longer in denial.

When Rose returned home, she confirmed that her daughter had a bun in the oven. Clare was in tears and locked herself in her room.

Rose walked with Paul and updated him on their daughter's situation. She explained her recent discovery, the test, and a quick assessment of their options.

Arkansas did not allow abortion, and none of the surrounding states did either. The closest state where they could confidently get an abortion at this point in the pregnancy seemed to be Illinois – which was a long way away.

Rose might be able to obtain some abortion pills, but it seemed too late in Clare's pregnancy to risk that solution.

Rose lamented that Clare would just have to have this baby. Paul was doing his best to keep up with the conversation and clearly struggled to process everything Rose had just apprised him of.

He didn't want to raise the suggestion of terminating this pregnancy with Clare; that option was just too dangerous and unnecessary. He also assured Rose they could raise this child if Clare wasn't up to the task. He thought having a baby in the family would be a manageable blessing.

These insights irritated Rose, and she was reluctant to simply accept the fact that it was too late to stop this pregnancy. Yet, she too believed that she and Paul could raise this child if Clare wasn't up to the task. She warmed to the notion.

By the time they returned home, Claire had left her room and was sitting with Della at the dining table. The two were discussing the wonder of childbirth, and Rose and Paul sat down next to them to listen to the discussion.

A Lucky Break Two
May 2037

E acher called Jenny, who interrupted a meeting to take his call. He quickly described the situation and the urgency of what was about to happen. She asked them to stay away from the fight and promised to get some help. Eacher and Irene discussed the situation and decided to turn around and go back to the plant. Perhaps they could safely observe from a distance.

As they approached the plant again, they could hear an exchange of gunfire. Bob was on the roof of the main building, using his M-16 to shoot at the bikers on the ground. Those riders were furious but in disarray. They were riding wildly around the site. Two more individuals arrived on the bridge, shooting toward the motorcycles roaming the power plant yard.

After about an hour, a Coast Guard helicopter swooped down from above. Several people with rifles fired at the motorcycles out the open cargo door of the chopper.

The motorcycles rallied and headed out the gate together. The helicopter followed them for some distance shooting. The bikes fled away at considerable speed.

The helicopter returned to the power plant and landed on the roof where Bob had been shooting. The blast of wind almost pushed him off the roof, but he was holding on tightly to a steel vent pipe poking through the roof.

Eacher and Irene drove into the plant and were joined by the two shooters from the bridge and two women union members who had just arrived. They all moved to the roof to discuss the situation. Irene called the President and gave her an update.

Jenny turned the situation over to her homeland security team, and they promised to coordinate with the state to defend this generating facility.

Eacher put her on speaker, and she promised Bob and his crew that she would order Maryland to make this power plant operational again. The defenders cheered when they heard her announcement.

Hoping the danger had passed, Eacher, Irene, and their engineer crossed the Potomac and took a different route back to Washington DC. They didn't want to take the chance that they might meet this gang on the road along the route they had initially taken.

They couldn't escape noticing the level of industrialization of the landscape along the road back to Washington DC. There were numerous wind turbines along the coast and along the Potomac. Furthermore, vast arrays of solar panels were erected between small farming operations. Eacher had spent some time in this portion of the country growing up and couldn't get over how different it looked now.

One of the more bucolic parts of the country would soon simply be a graveyard for renewable electrical generation equipment. Since more than half of the wind turbines were still generating electricity, it was too early to make that claim. Yet, Eacher did not doubt that within ten, or in a few places, twenty years, all these wind turbines and fields of solar panels would simply be rusting relics of a failed energy transition.

Over the next two months, two more fossil-fueled power plants on long-term standby were destroyed. Others had long ago been gutted of their copper and other metals. The survival of this power plant was much more critical than either Eacher or Irene had recognized initially. There had been no improvement in the electrical system since Jenny took office.

***

Jenny met with Walter Iverson, the most recent Chairman of the Board of the Morgantown Plant, and asked him why they were not producing electricity now that natural gas prices were at much lower levels.

He pointed out that when the plant was first constructed, it was a moneymaker. As designed, it attained high utilization rates and made a decent return on capital.

However, with the increase in wind and solar electrical generation, they were forced to play second fiddle. The wind and solar developers had pricing preferences and subsidy advantages that allowed them to get paid whenever they produced electricity. Most reliable power plants had been relegated to a very inefficient backup role. They limped by for a while with the help of government subsidies and then were pushed out of the market entirely with the government's insistence. With the end of the carbon tax, they had simply returned to their previous situation, where they were still in financial trouble.

"What would it take to return to your glory days when you used to make money?" Jenny asked.

"Just stop penalizing us."

"That's it?" Jenny asked.

"Stop making us capture all of our carbon dioxide emissions. That alone makes our electricity generation much more expensive."

"I'll take a look into that."

"Let us produce our electricity on a level playing field."

"How so?"

"When we have to constantly adjust our output to provide only the electricity that the wind turbines and solar panels aren't providing at the moment, we're at a huge disadvantage."

"Is that really happening?"

"It wasn't before the grid flooded with wind and solar power. We had no problems producing very inexpensive electricity by ourselves."

"So we should get rid of the solar and wind power?"

"Not at all. Just make those renewable sources partner with other generators to provide reliable power. They could team up with energy storage systems or even peaking power plants. Don't let their unreliability be the central feature of our electricity system."

"And that's all you need?" Jenny said.

"You work that out with our local electrical network management office, and we'll have this plant back online in thirty days after you sort it out."

"You got the fuel?"

"I'm pretty sure we can get it. Deal?"

"Done," Jenny said. She directed the Department of Energy to sort it out for this one power plant and turned them loose.

Within ninety days, this plant was online and operating at close to an average of eighty percent capacity utilization; during peak usage periods, it approached a hundred percent. This natural gas combined cycle power plant provided a stable backbone of power for this electrical network and several others that were connected.

The existing wind and solar plants filed a lawsuit and did their best to get the Morgantown power generation shut down. In the meantime, the regional electrical system improved considerably in a specific region of Maryland.

In time, she encouraged several natural gas, coal, and even nuclear power plants to return to operation on essentially the same terms. With the new rules, a couple of developers even brought new plants online.

Oval Office Visits
June 2037

Jenny wanted to reopen as many airports as possible, but the logistics and business challenges were onerous. Most of these airports were considered temporarily closed, at least until some sort of new biologically friendly airplane fuel could be utilized. An unutilized airport quickly falls into disrepair, and the staff to run it does not hang around waiting for it to return to service.

Furthermore, as the runways closed, small farmers moved onto the adjacent land and started farming crops. To add insult to injury, a few wind turbines appeared at several former airports and now blocked some of the landing strips.

Some former terminals were broken into and were then occupied by squatters. The utilities were no longer turned on at these airports. Hence, the bathrooms quickly resembled those where other transients had taken over.

Her advisors indicated that it made sense to initially open only one airport in the Washington DC, area. Ronald Reagan Washington National Airport had been chosen for this role. Work to restore operations had been underway for the past three months.

Jenny stood on the tarmac next to Mr. Lee. They stood in the baggage handling area in an open area where a plane could park. Her secret service agents vigilantly guarded her. At their insistence, she wore a bulletproof vest under her coat. This visit was unannounced, which her team believed was the best way to confound a potential sniper.

As head of the airport restoration initiative, Mr. Lee tried to update her on his progress. He had previously run an airport in South Korea and was considered very knowledgeable.

"How soon will this airport be back in operation?" Jenny asked the nervous Mr. Lee, who was fidgeting with his clipboard.

"It's already operational." He said flatly, seemingly anxious to move on to his next task.

"Really? That's great! How many planes have landed here?"

"Since we reopened the airport?"

"Yes."

"Two." He said.

"Just two?"

"That's a lot considering the difficulty of securing and storing acceptable jet fuel."

"Is that something you're personally managing?"

"No, actually, I let the airlines arrange it for themselves. We don't have the insurance to protect ourselves if we accidentally fuel a jet with defective fuel."

"Makes sense. How's that going?"

"The major challenge is that the jet fuel pipeline that used to serve the airport is no longer in service. It took a while to clean out the fuel storage tanks, and then fuel trucks had to run continuously to fill them."

"So, which airline took the lead?"

"Air China has been the main driver. Their team flew in on one of the aircraft and has been busily working to allow a plane to travel from Beijing twice a week. Their staff is currently living in that plane hangar." He pointed to a nearby building. "They cleaned out the squatters who had been living there."

Jenny noticed clotheslines outside the hangar where Chinese faces were drying their laundry. "Are the Chinese also restoring the computer systems for flght operations?"

"No, I'm afraid that's something we can't entrust to a single airline. We've got a top-tier air traffic controller consultant coordinating those systems on behalf of the airport authority."

"That sounds encouraging."

"Well, it shouldn't. The computer program is simply too large for the tiny operation that we'll be running initially. Also, since almost no other public airports are in operation, our pilots are flying mostly blind around the country."

"Is it safe?"

"Every operation involves a risk, especially when so few recent standard operating procedures are in place. We'll initially limit the number of aircraft to three a week and expand as time and demand allows. Few Americans can afford to fly at this point, and we may struggle to fill the seats on even a few planes."

"So, what time is the flight scheduled to land today?"

"Between two and three pm. We don't have long to wait at this point."

Jenny thanked him for his insights and was escorted to the landing tower.

She discussed flight operations while monitoring the runway from her elevated perch. At that moment, the electricity went out, and a noisy generator could be heard starting up. The lights returned.

"Does that happen often?" Jenny asked.

"Off and on. We don't have the budget to pay the more expensive electricity rates, so we have a backup generator in emergencies. If we didn't have that flight on the schedule, the generators would not have started."

At this moment, an airplane appeared in the distance. One of the flight controllers spoke with the pilot, and they listened as another flight controller used his air traffic controller scope to guide them to the ground. The Qatar Airways plane landed smoothly and taxied in their direction. The ground was a little uneven, and the plane jerked back and forth noticeably as it approached the area where they had been standing before.

A ground staff member used flags to park the plane on the tarmac, and then a set of stairs was rolled up alongside. The plane's door opened, and the first passengers emerged. They headed down the stairs and then waited for their bags to be offloaded from the plane.

Meanwhile, the workers who had parked the plane rushed over to open the plane's baggage compartment with another steel structure. Bags were being moved into a pile next to the plane. When the passengers recognized their own gear, porters would grab it and carry it out through a side runway gate where shuttle buses and taxis were waiting. The plane seemed about half full of passengers.

Jenny smiled broadly and gave the employees a "thumbs up" sign. This airport was back in business.

***

The initial visitors were diplomatic, but several airlines followed with business travelers seeking to capitalize on the changes in the United States.

As it worked out, the first business people that Jenny met with several weeks later were executives from companies that had once been major US energy companies. They were still large and successful companies, though they now conducted most of their operations abroad and had relocated their headquarters outside the United States. Since global oil prices were almost entirely determined by OPEC these oil and gas companies needed to stay closely tuned to the cartel's intentions. There were numerous corporate headquarters now located in Doha, Qatar.

"President Almond, thank you for allowing us to meet with you." Bubba Smith, the Senior Executive Vice President of one of the three largest diversified oil and gas companies, initiated the conversation with a thick Southern accent. He was a senior executive with a goofy toupee that didn't blend well with the natural hair growing along the side of his head. He was about average height and seriously overweight.

"Mr. Smith, it's nice to meet you. How can I assist?" Jenny replied.

"Well, my company wanted me to meet with you to better understand how you see the current situation developing. As you are almost certainly aware, we lost much money when the government shut down most of our operations in the United States. The carbon tax was, of course, the final death knoll. Still, you need to understand that even before that happened, the regulatory environment had gotten so toxic that we were already two-blocked. Getting a permit to drill a well was essentially impossible. There were no federal lease sales for either onshore or offshore wells. It was also illegal to flare any natural gas, even for wildcat wells where we weren't sure we'd discover hydrocarbons where we were drilling; it might take us years before we'd be allowed to build a gathering system for any successful discoveries."

"And now you want to know if the time is right to return to the United States?" Jenny asked.

"That's not really why I'm here," Bubba said. "The good news was that we never completely left. I wanted to go over our *special deal* with the US government. While the carbon tax raised the gasoline prices that ordinary Americans paid, we negotiated an exemption. We could avoid those taxes as long as we provided it for the benefit of the government or shipped it internationally and shared our profits with the US Treasury."

"So that's why the government could keep operating most of its fossil fuel vehicle fleet?" Jenny asked, suggesting she should have known but didn't.

"Well, actually, it was more involved than that. If the government decided to support a business, like the Post Office or the relocation business, that also allowed us to provide gasoline and diesel to them without paying the carbon taxes."

"There can't be much production left."

"There's more than you would guess. But, the beauty of our last arrangement with the government was that it allowed us to keep our pilot light going. We could continue to protect some of our leases, operate our pipeline facilities, and even maintain a portion of our refineries. They even allowed us to use some of our liquefaction facilities to sell Liquefied Natural Gas abroad; that concession cost us most of our profits."

"So, if we can reverse the rules that slowed you down, you might be able to ramp up your drilling and refining activities again?" Jenny asked hopefully.

"Well, it's not quite that simple. The global oil supply is mostly controlled by OPEC. The citizens in the countries with the highest productivity can afford to pay world prices for gasoline, diesel, and jet fuel. Unfortunately, most of those in the United States are no longer in the front of this line." Bubba said.

"So, why are you here?" Jenny asked.

"We'd like your assurances that our deal with the last government still stands. The contract ended right after the last election."

"You understand that you're free to produce and sell as much as you want without worrying about carbon taxes?" Jenny asked. "Most onshore leases are privately owned and don't involve the government."

"True, but I can't assure you that any additional oil produced domestically will be sold here. Users in Asia will be clamoring for it."

"Look, I understand that without the carbon tax, our various governments no longer need a special deal with your company. The various levels of government are now just ordinary customers. If they can afford it, they can buy it. Produce what you want and sell all you can. It's not my job to limit how you conduct your business."

"You can get the most restrictive environmental rules removed?"

"We'll aim at the ones solely designed to inhibit your ability to operate. Give me a list, and we'll do our best to help. Just don't cut corners on things that really matter. I don't want any more superfund sites."

Bubba looked serious for a moment. "There are a ton of such regulations and permitting constraints. Some predate the carbon taxes, and others were added later to further impair our operations. I'll send you that list."

"That will help. We'll get to those rules as fast as we can. Worst case, I'll simply waive enforcement of the most painful and then pardon you if another part of our federal government tries to penalize you."

"That would be mighty kind. However, let me be clear about one detail. There is a lot of 'country risk' in the United States according to our investors. If your administration gets replaced next election, we'll face a pretty hostile environment."

"We need to demonstrate to our citizens that we're on the right path by the end of my term. Otherwise, all bets are off," Jenny said.

"An honest answer. I'll discuss it with our board. We have plenty of other countries where we can invest our capital."

"No doubt. Thanks for coming. One of my assistants will give you my business card and escort you out of the building."

Just after those remarks, a member of Jenny's staff escorted Mr. Smith out a side door in the Oval Office. As he left, a Chinese oil and gas company executive was being led into her office. The timing was not accidental.

"Yes, sir," Bubba said to a junior executive on their way out. "We need to *get* while the getting's good."

Later that day, Jenny met with a panel of executives from industrial farming concerns. She started the meeting by confirming that food security was one of her top priorities. People needed to believe they did not have to grow their own food. Otherwise, they would hesitate to return to other employment.

She thanked the visitors for their cooperation with her Homeland Security agency. This particular group played a vital role in restoring the soup kitchens to service.

They seemed impressed that Jenny knew as much about that arrangement as she did, but they also seemed a little uncomfortable with that insight.

Jenny clarified that the federal government was not interested in purchasing imported food to distribute to food-challenged regions. However, the food importers could do whatever they wanted to compete in this country. She thought expanding their output was a good idea for these organizations and others.

They asked whether she would restrict them from selling their food abroad.

She assured them they could sell whatever they wanted, to whomever they wanted. Furthermore, she would endeavor to eliminate any other crippling government requirements that would impact their ability to conduct their business. She asked them to send her a list of their concerns.

They were particularly worried about transportation restrictions. Studies had been done that suggested that transporting food long distances consumes a lot of oil. A single tomato shipped from California to the East Coast was reputed to require as much as four ounces of oil in transit. If that were true, these high costs would put those growers at an economic disadvantage compared to the local farmers. To further ensure that outcome, the last administration had insisted on layering even more costs on any efforts to transport food long distances.

She thought that such modifications were already being addressed and wished them success.

As they left her office, an executive from an Indian food company was waiting to enter her office. While they weren't introduced, the gentleman now going into her office was well known on television commercials that had recently been aired.

A Carpetbagger
August 2037

From a distance, Paul noticed a vehicle pull up to the front gate. It was a snub-nosed luxury electric vehicle made in China. Beautifully made and very quiet, he hadn't seen another car this fancy in the past ten years.

The driver appeared to be Hispanic. He was dressed in a chauffeur uniform and wore a military-style pistol belt with a revolver at his side. As the driver emerged from the car and walked toward the house through the unlocked front gate, Della left her seat on the porch and met him just inside the gate. They greeted each other in Spanish.

The passenger then opened a rear door and headed towards the house. He was a middle-aged man of Asian descent. He wore expensive trousers, a crew neck shirt, leather sandals, and a stylish wide-brimmed hat.

When he saw Della, he instinctively gave her a disparaging glance but then caught himself and said something akin to, "Are either of your parents home?"

Della pointed toward the crops.

Paul stepped out of the house a few seconds later and walked crisply toward the visitors.

The passenger gave him a smile.

"Paul, we have a guest," Della said.

"Nice to meet you," Paul said. "What brings you to this neck of the woods?"

"Just arrived on a flight from China."

"Wow, that's the first time I've heard anyone say something like that in a long time."

"Yeah, sure beats a slow boat."

"No doubt. How can we help?"

"Just seeing if the owner might be interested in selling this land to me. I'm buying some acreage for my investors."

"I doubt if that's of interest, but we can discuss that idea with my wife."

Della left the men to their discussion and returned to the house.

Paul texted Rose on her mobile phone. "Guests. Come to the front gate."

Rose showed up about five minutes later.

"Rose, I want to introduce you to Mr..."

"My name is ZhuMing, just call me Ming. Nice to meet you."

"Yes, thanks for visiting us. Is there something that I can help with?" Rose asked.

"I represent a Chinese investment company buying land in the United States. Interested in selling?"

"Well, that would depend on what you're offering."

"Tell me a little bit more about what you own?"

"We own five acres." Rose motioned around the area as she described various elements. "The house and barn are on this part of the parcel, and the acres we manage are right over there."

"What are you asking for it?"

Paul listened closely. At this point, the driver returned to the car, leaving ZhuMing to his negotiations.

"Ming, our homestead is really valuable."

"I can understand why you would say that. This is such a beautiful area, and you've done much work. My problem is that I must stay within my budget for my investors. I couldn't offer you anything close to its worth."

"Why is that?" Paul interrupted with a hint of disappointment.

"Well, I'm afraid it's all based on the economic value involved. What's the value of the food you could grow on your acreage? Maybe thirty thousand dollars a year?"

"Maybe something like that." Rose looked at her fields. It was a primitive-looking operation with lots of weeds.

"How much of that food would be left over after you fed your family."

"Well, maybe none of it," Rose replied.

"So, what would be the value of us owning this land?" Ming asked.

"Well, I assume that if you bought it, you'd want to live here."

"No, I'm sorry, my family is in China."

"Then why are you here in our country looking for land to acquire?"

"I believe our investors can make a decent return with this type of acreage."

"How?"

"Land is still scarce in China, and this land is both a bet on America and cropland. These are two areas that my wealthy investors understand quite well."

"Well, we don't make much in the United States anymore. It makes sense that this rich bottomland would still be valuable."

"I don't disagree with you."

"You'd want us to stay and operate everything?"

"Well, that depends on how qualified you are as tenants. You have an operational tractor?"

"No."

"You've got irrigation?"

"Not for our new acreage yet, but we're working on it."

"You've got natural gas?" Ming asked.

"No. There are no natural gas distribution lines in this neighborhood," Paul interjected, partly to remind them that he was still there.

"Then what you're telling me is that you've essentially got a subsistence operation. Hard to love."

It was difficult to argue with this assessment; it was close to the mark. "Well, you've got a point, but you have to value it not from the way it now stands but based on the improvements that can be made now that the country is getting back on its feet," Rose said.

"I'll tell you what, take my card, and call me when the improvements you describe materialize. I'll come back and make an offer at that time."

"Well, in the meantime, be advised that things are not always as they appear," Rose said. "We know of two properties nearby where the owners died. We've faced some violent squatters that took over that acreage."

"We've seen similar things happening all over the place. Which properties are those, by the way?"

"It's not for us to say." Paul cut Rose off from responding.

"Well, it could be lucrative if you did. The county is sometimes willing to foreclose homesteads for unpaid property taxes. It would be worth it to us to learn about such situations before they go public."

"Why?" Paul asked.

"If we know of owners with unpaid property taxes before the government gives them notice, we're in position to cut a deal without competition. We might even allow such owners or squatters to remain around for a while."

"But the squatters wouldn't have clear title."

"We'd work to locate the real owners – or their heirs – and then cut an even better deal with those title holders. Here's my card if you know of anything that might interest us. If your referral results in a deal, we'll pay you a small commission."

This was the closest thing to a job Paul had gotten wind of for some time. Grinning, he took the card and gingerly placed it in his pocket. "Nice meeting you. Can you share a sample commission agreement with me for my review?"

Ming took his email address and promised to send one. He then turned around and walked back to his car. He glanced around the area, shook his head in disappointment, and climbed into the back seat. His driver smoothly turned the car around and then drove away at a leisurely pace.

"Our first carpetbaggers!" Rose said after he'd left.

"Glad I got a chance to meet him. That almost sounded like an employment offer! Things might be looking up!" Paul said, reaching into his pocket to confirm that he still had Ming's business card. He squeezed it between his fingers to prove it was still there. *Time to get to work!*

Wheels Up
August 2037

Paul and Rose discussed the possibility that he could serve as a bird dog for Ming's investments.

Rose wasn't against him getting a position. With the addition of Jose and Della, there was enough labor to handle all the farming requirements. They needed to cover property taxes, or they would get evicted. It was imperative to find a way to generate some outside income.

However, in terms of helping Ming, an inescapable issue was at stake. Their temporary friends deserved to squat as long as they could – even if there were people like Ming ready to pounce the moment they appeared on the unpaid property tax list. In fact, the decent thing to do was for Paul and Rose to inform all their neighbors to pay the property taxes as long as they resided on that land. Rose insisted he find something else to pursue, and Paul redirected his job search.

Paul didn't have many contacts that would be able to offer him employment; otherwise, he would have already been in touch. Yet there was one he hadn't tried. Gus, the truck driver who had driven his brother and wife back and forth to Houston, put them to work on two trips. *Perhaps he might have some ideas?* Paul called him immediately.

Gus pointed out that he was no longer in the moving business but indicated that drivers were in demand. He asked Paul if he was interested in a position.

Paul quickly accepted, and Gus promised to grab him later in the week.

Rose was not particularly pleased that Paul would go on the road, but they needed the income.

Two days later, Gus called Paul when thirty minutes away. Paul quickly threw his last few items in a duffle bag and let Rose know he was leaving.

She and the kids had been working on their hands and knees in the field, and they quickly headed to the gate to say goodbye. Caked in dirt, Paul met them at the entrance as they waited for his ride.

A few minutes later, a large truck came into view. Driving an eighteen-wheeler transport truck loaded with a mix of Chinese pickup trucks and SUVs, he pulled off the shoulder slightly and coasted to a stop.

With the engine still running, Gus rolled down the window and directed Paul to throw his bag between the seats. Paul gave Rose and the kids a firm but quick hug, opened the passenger door, and climbed into the cab. Paul waved out the window to his loved ones as the truck moved forward slowly. Gus then returned to the right traffic lane and then set his cruise control to a speed that was about fifteen miles over the posted speed limit. Paul paid close attention to his every move.

It had been warm outside, and Paul was dressed in shorts and a T-shirt. Gus had the air conditioner cranked up high, and Paul needed to pull a sweatshirt out of his gear.

Gus had notified his company, and they had already confirmed that Paul now had a position; they'd finish his paperwork when he arrived at one of their offices.

Paul was ecstatic; it was the feeling that a college graduate got when they started their first job. But like that college student, he didn't understand what exactly he'd be doing and feared that there were better candidates with experience that might still show up. Gus walked him through all the aspects of being a truck driver and Paul asked many questions.

These trucks were critical to an economic recovery. Since trucks were scarce, they needed drivers to work in shifts to keep the limited number of vehicles on the road. There were fewer drivers in the system than Paul would have guessed. Many potential drivers were tethered to small farms and were hard to locate or interact with. In addition, Gus pointed out that gangs and pirates had been actively stealing cargo.

"Pirates?"

"You know, idiots and criminals on motorcycles trying to hijack our loads. It happened to me once. The bastards stole a loaded fuel truck that I had been driving."

"A fuel truck! Did they surprise you at a stoplight?"

"Nope, they caught me on the Interstate armed with shotguns and explosives. They forced me to stop by threatening to throw dynamite under my truck. They also knocked me out when I complied."

"Damn. That's terrifying."

"Which is why you now have a position. You need courage, but more importantly, you need to be able to think on your feet." Gus told him the whole story of the attack on his vehicle. He was convinced that the real problem was driving on a highway where they hung out.

"So, now you're taking back roads?"

"You got it."

"Would it make sense to drive at night?"

"That's a good driving shift to work, especially after midnight. The point is that you want to make it as inconvenient as possible for the bad guys to locate you and take action to intercept you."

Gus continued to share as much as he could. Paul had been in the dark before accepting this job, and now he wondered if he'd been too hasty.

When Gus arrived in Shreveport, Paul better understood what was expected of him. He was apprehensive about what he'd likely face on the highways.

Gus drove his vehicle to a local vehicle dealership. The sales lot was surrounded by tall fences topped by concertina wire.

The two of them got out of the truck. Gus personally offloaded the vehicles from the transport and signed an acceptance document with the manager.

Gus drove Paul to a nearby dispatch office. He then turned the vehicle over to another operator, who was tasked with driving it to its next job.

Gus caught another truck that evening, and Paul didn't run into him again for a few months.

Paul remained at the dispatch office and received training videos and driving instructions from one of the staff members.

On the third day, Paul was tasked with driving a fuel truck from Shreveport back to the port in Houston. The tank was empty, so it should be less of a target than a fully loaded truck. Thirty minutes later, the transport arrived at the dispatch center.

The departing driver was about six foot two, thin, and middle-aged. He looked like he hadn't slept in a week. He nervously chain-smoked cigarettes, and his hands were shaking as he handed Paul the keys.

"Anything I need to know about this vehicle?"

The outgoing driver just chuckled and shook his head. "Return her to the Houston port. The map is in the glove box, along with the credit card for your fuel. Make sure the dispatcher here gets your next of kin info."

"When does it have to be there?" Paul asked.

"The sooner the better. The head office will start docking your pay if it's not there by midnight." The previous driver turned and walked towards the bathroom.

Paul couldn't believe that this was really happening. Just the idea of driving a truck this large unnerved him. The little training he'd gone through hardly qualified him for anything. Even so, his growing family needed the money, and no one seemed concerned about his lack of truck-driving experience. They apparently required bodies, not experts. It sounded a bit like trench warfare.

He approached the truck, climbed into the cabin, and threw his gear onto the passenger seat. The truck's fuel tank was topped off, and he let it idle while he examined the map. He picked a route, cranked up the music, and rolled down the window. He followed some residential roads through a few neighborhoods. Then he found some country dirt and gravel roads headed in roughly the right direction.

He'd hardly seen a vehicle on many red clay dirt roads he'd been riding on. Had he followed the Interstate, he could have made the trip in about four hours. Given his choice of routes, he made the trip in eleven hours and rarely found himself on either an asphalt or concrete road. The weather had been dry recently, and wet roads weren't a problem on this trip. He dropped the truck off just before midnight.

He was given the nickname Hokey Pokey by the dispatcher that accepted his vehicle.

They encouraged him to get some sleep. He'd pick up his next truck the following morning around 7 am. They pointed him to a back room with cots.

He was back in the dispatch office around 6:30 in the morning, and someone handed him a sandwich from one of the vending machines. This time, his instructions were quite different. He was now being tasked to drive a genuinely crappy van. It had artwork on the side that suggested it was owned by a famous tequila company, and there were about a half dozen wooden crates in the cargo portion of the vehicle. It spewed smoke clouds out the rear exhaust. The cab floor and dashboard were decorated with a shag carpet. This time, he was given specific instructions that he was required to drive up Interstate 45 to Dallas and needed to start his trip within the hour. If anyone pursued him, he would pull over immediately and not try to escape. They clarified that it was not a problem if he was required to surrender his cargo.

After a quick trip to the bathroom, he climbed into the van and made his way directly to the highway. He had barely passed The Woodlands, about forty miles north of central Houston, when a group of motorcycles passed on his left side and motioned for him to pull his vehicle over.

He did so and followed their instructions as they investigated his load. When they opened the wooden boxes, they were full of quart-sized tequila bottles. A large and particularly scary-looking biker took a swig and made eyes like it was the best thing he'd ever tasted. The other bikers also took a drink and seemed to think it was something special. They called in their discovery and asked Paul to follow them with the truck. He did so, and when he arrived at some sort of meeting area about halfway to Dallas, they offloaded all of his crates.

Paul was allowed to drive off with his van. He was stopped twice more on the way to Dallas, and each time, he explained where he had offloaded the liquor.

They listened closely to Paul's story when he got to his destination. They had no particular concerns about the lost cargo. They pointed him toward one of the back rooms where he could sleep.

The following morning, Paul woke up to what looked like an invasion of drivers. Thirty vehicles had driven from Houston to Dallas the previous evening. All had high value loads of fuel, ammunition, and passenger vehicles. They had left as a convoy about one in the morning and arrived before dawn. They were all slapping each other on the back and congratulating Paul for planting the alcohol in the enemy camp.

When the trucks had driven with their lights off past the point where Paul had offloaded the liquor, there was a bonfire raging and loud music. Some of the drivers claimed to have also noticed scantily clad women dancing wildly at the party. It apparently was quite an outing.

The remaining vehicles were quickly unloaded in the area and he returned to Houston in their convoy a few hours later.

Honey, I'm Home
September 2037

It had been a long day. Eacher and Irene sat through various government weather-related meetings, during which the establishment scientists in attendance repeatedly assured them that global temperatures were soaring. It was the type of claim rolled out for the gullible and the faithful; in his experience, it always disintegrated under a thousand questions upon closer examination.

Even the term of art for the decarbonization crusade rarely used the term "global warming" in recent decades. Instead, politicians did their best to repurpose the term "climate change" which before recent centuries had only been subject to natural influences. The official meaning going forward, however, was that climate change was now caused primarily by manmade influences.

Jenny had made it clear. Neither Eacher nor Irene were to engage or upset believers in the Catastrophic Anthropogenic Global Warming (CAGW) hypothesis. On several points, Irene started to respond and Eacher bit his lower lip which was their signal to reconsider what the other was about to say.

When they later met privately with Jenny, Irene outlined what she thought was going on. The rural weather data, special-purpose satellites, and weather balloons indicated that the most recent global temperature anomaly was flat. The only outlier was claimed in a very subjective Surface Temperature database. There was nothing to be alarmed about.

Jenny wanted confirmation from an outside source.

Eacher sent Windy an email message to see what the Chinese might be willing to share from their technical vantage

117

point. The Chinese either built or owned most of the satellites that now monitored Earth's atmosphere from space. With a bit of luck, he would have a response in his inbox when he logged in the following morning.

Windy's rise into a position of influence in China was mainly based on her activities while in the United States. She had sought Chinese assistance to exploit certain newsworthy materials that Eacher and Irene had uncovered. Jenny's election impressed those in her country who were aware of her efforts.

After returning to China, certain Communist Party officials determined that her country could take advantage of Windy's connections. She took some time off after having a baby but afterwards, was hired by her government as a liaison to the United States. She and Paul's brother, Kirk, now lived in a high-rise apartment building in Beijing.

As Eacher opened the door to his apartment, the phone rang. He answered it, thinking it was Windy. He was taken aback when he heard Jasmine's voice. He cursed himself for not looking at his screen before he answered the call. His immediate thought was relief that Irene had not yet returned from the office.

"Honey, I'm glad I caught you!" Jasmine said.

"No problem. Is everything okay at my place?"

"Yes, your neighbor loaded me up with some of his crops. There is enough food there to last the winter."

"So, you'll be fine then?"

"Well, I would be if I had stayed."

"What do you mean?" Eacher said a bit icily, now riveted to what he feared she would say next. "Where are you now?"

"I'm in Washington DC," she said. "Not far from where you live."

"Why would you come here? You should have been fine at my place."

"Oh honey, I can't thank you enough for allowing me to stay at *our* house, but, you know, if we're going to continue our relationship, we should live together again."

"How did you get here?"

"I was able to catch a ride with another traveler, but I couldn't think of a better time to reconnect with you."

"So you're really here in the capital?" Eacher voiced this with a tone that was less than encouraging.

"Darling, I came a long way to see you! Would you mind picking me up to discuss the situation over dinner?"

"I'm sorry, where are you now?"

"I'm about a mile from your place. If picking me up is a problem, I've got enough money for a cab; just give me your address."

Irene walked in and noticed him on the phone. She gave him an inquisitive look as if to ask who he was speaking with.

Eacher pointed to his cell phone and then pointed to the sky, suggesting that it was someone he needed to talk to. Given their jobs, it might even be the President.

She went into the kitchen and started moving some pots around. Eacher guessed she was straining to hear his part of the discussion.

"Text me your address, and I'll come get you." He whispered.

She started to respond, but Eacher had already hung up on her. She had what she needed, and there was no purpose in continuing the discussion.

Eacher went into the kitchen. "Irene, I've just been called back into the office. Can you fend for dinner for yourself?"

"Eacher, would you like for me to go with you? Whatever you're working on probably includes me."

"You're right, it does." He said with some assurance. "But this is an issue I need to fix alone. I'll fill you in when I return." He walked out of the kitchen and quickly left their apartment. He wasn't sure if he meant these remarks, but it seemed like the right thing to say so that she wouldn't be concerned.

What to do? He feared something like this might happen. *Why didn't I explain this to Irene? What's next?*

Eacher climbed into his small government sedan and slowly drove it out of the parking garage. Before he entered the street, he looked at his text messages to confirm where she was. He drove slowly, trying to force his brain to come up with an acceptable solution.

When Jasmine first married him, he seemed like a catch. He was young, good-looking, and taught at a major university. She was beautiful but also intelligent and stylish. She voiced a willingness to do whatever it took to advance his career.

He had always wanted children, and Jasmine had been somewhat coy during their courtship, intimating that she had no objections. Even so, she always insisted that the timing was wrong after they were married. Eacher struggled to remember the specifics but he could only recall generalities, with one exception. The last few days had become a cattle brand seared on his brain.

She made no secret that she thought his devotion to scientific rigor was a selfish indulgence and regularly pointed out that opinion. From her vantage, his professional determination and persistence against mainstream notions had cost him his tenure. That failure had denied both of them the little house with the white picket fence at an Ivy League College filled with children and pets. In her mind, the blame for the failure of their relationship was clearly on his shoulders.

Eacher had intended to play the primary breadwinner role, something his academic rejections had impeded years later. He especially needed his wife's support after his change in circumstances. Yet that was the time she chose to leave. It felt more like a betrayal than a breakup. He felt used and doubted whether she had ever loved him.

He now regretted that they hadn't had kids soon after marriage. While their eventual breakup would have tapped him to fund his children's expenses, he'd have stayed in touch with his kids and, through them, had more ties with his ex-wife. It wouldn't have made them friends, but it would have forged them into an extended family structure.

Absent all those connections that might have been, he was driving to meet a woman who, in many ways, was a stranger. Whatever love he had once felt for her was difficult to recollect.

Eacher drove to the restaurant address she had texted. He pulled down his car's visor to shield his eyes from the sun. She wore a light blue cotton dress with a matching straw hat and stood next to a large suitcase on the sidewalk in the shadow of the building.

She appeared not to recognize him when he drove up. It had been many years since they had seen each other; he was much thinner, and his hair had turned gray.

He waved at her, and her face lit up. He then parallel-parked along the curb, exited the car, and quickly relocked the doors as she moved to the passenger side. Before she could open the door, he was standing next to her. She looked at him uncertainly – trying to read his expression and determine his mood. Without saying a word, he grasped the handle on her suitcase and wheeled it towards the restaurant entrance. She trailed close behind. Together, they seemed to be a couple that did not speak much. The hostess greeted them and sat them together at a booth.

Jasmine looked nervous. Her suitcase was sitting next to her in the booth, and she was very protective of it. Eacher speculated that it contained everything she owned.

"Thanks for coming, my love; it's been a while."

He had intended to be gentle with her, but what came out was more direct than intended. "Why are you here? We separated years ago and have hardly spoken since. Your suggestion that we should be together again after all this time is difficult to comprehend."

"Eacher, look, I know I've surprised you. You never would have invited me up here."

"I'm sorry, but that's true. I've got my own life now."

"I know, and I'm glad for your success. It's been a tough world for a woman my age."

"How have you gotten by?" Eacher asked. He was more than a bit curious about what she had been doing. When she didn't respond, he continued. "It doesn't appear you've spent much time in the sun. You still look good, by the way."

"Well, thank you for noticing. When we separated, I moved in with my mother. I worked locally in minor advertising jobs and monitored Mom's finances. When she passed, I inherited the house and what was left of her savings. I worked as a volunteer at the church and maintained a small garden. I was able to feed myself until recently." She paused for about a minute, then said. "I made a mistake leaving you and have regretted it since."

"It's reassuring to hear you say that, but that was long ago. We went our different ways." Eacher said softly. While waiting for her response, he took a quick glimpse at the menu.

"You've been right about so many things. The country fell apart, as you predicted. Despite that, you seem to have landed on your feet. You're so much smarter than I realized. I'd like to be on your team again."

"So your concerns are primarily financial?" Eacher still couldn't believe she was suggesting he'd ever been right about anything. To now be willing to suggest that he had achieved success smacked of desperation on her part, though hearing it induced a feeling of vindication. Even so, he remembered that her advertising background made her skilled at saying the right things to sell ideas.

"Eacher, it's more than money. I need an anchor for my life. Someone to grow old with. Someone to care if anything happens to me."

"Yes, but why me? You're still pretty enough you could have found someone else to commit to."

"You really think so?"

"Yes. However, I'm afraid I'm already in a relationship. If you signed the divorce papers years ago, neither of us would even consider getting back together."

"Does your being here suggest that you're having doubts about your other relationship?"

"Look, when you left, it flattened me. You left me in a deep emotional hole that was difficult to escape."

The waitress came to their table. "Ready to order?"

"Yes, just give us a few more minutes," Eacher said, placing the menu on his placemat.

The waitress had already given them fifteen minutes. She rolled her eyes, popped her gum, and headed away again.

Jasmine pulled out the menu. "I reckon I should eat the crow."

"Is that grilled or fried?"

"Blackened."

"Let's share it."

They finished dinner, and Eacher used his phone to arrange an inexpensive hotel for her. It had a two-star rating and catered to extended stays. They drove to the entrance, and he parked the car and carried her suitcase to the front desk. He used his credit card to cover the room charge and electricity deposit. She looked at him thankfully. "Would you mind carrying this to the room for me? My arm is tired."

"Really? You think someone would really fall for that?" Her room was on the first floor, down a short hallway, and he pulled the bag behind them.

She opened the door with the room key. The room was worn out, and cheap motivational prints were on the wall. The porcelain in the bathroom was stained, and the window screen had holes in it. It would be too expensive to run the air conditioning, at least it would be if Eacher were staying in the room. He couldn't stop Jasmine from doing anything she wanted, but he would talk to her about her budget for staying here in the coming days.

"Is it okay if I leave it here?" Eacher had placed it to the right of the dresser. When he turned, she was just in front of him.

"God, why do I want to kiss you?"

"That would make no sense," Eacher replied somewhat curtly. He wasn't that much of a catch for her to even make this offer.

Jasmine closed quickly on him and pressed her chest against him. Her lips followed. Eacher instinctively resisted, then stopped fighting her. He recalled them on their honeymoon for a second, but that image simply flashed, and then fled. She felt thin and firm, though he suspected her bra was doing a lot of work holding things in place. She pulled herself closer and leaned her head against his chest.

He was almost surprised that he felt no emotional or physical attraction. A particular tactile memory was triggered. He could vaguely remember similar embraces in their past. Yet, unlike a much younger version of himself, there was no imperative to consummate anything. He really just wanted to escape and get back to his apartment. "Jasmine, I'm not thirty years old anymore. This is about as far as I get, even with an attractive woman like you."

"That's okay. We can work on it."

"Actually, no, we can't. I'm in a relationship that I can't afford to jeopardize. Tell you what, spend a few days in this city and then take a bus back to my house in Arkansas. You can stay there until we move back." Eacher was already confident she would not follow his suggestion, but it had to be said.

"Kind of you," she said. Thanks for pretending that you still believe I'm attractive."

"No pretending there. You're a catch. Hope you meet someone who can give you what you want and need."

She gave him another kiss, and this one he anticipated, cut it short and headed to the door. He gave her one final glance. She still stood there anticipating his return. He exited the door.

He stopped by a restroom on his way out to wash off the smell of her perfume. The clerk gave him a curious look as he left the building, perhaps wondering why he was leaving so quickly. Eacher had the sense that many of their rooms were rented by the hour.

He drove back to his apartment, and Irene had already gone to bed. He quietly completed his bedtime preparations and quietly climbed into bed with her.

"Everything okay?" Irene murmured, half asleep.

"Yes, nothing to worry about."

She quickly returned to sleep, and he lay in bed wondering why the evening had gone as it had. He loved Irene. While he had once loved Jasmine, those emotions were long past. It was torture as old memories bubbled into his awareness, and he dreamed that they had never separated. He woke up anxious and reassured himself where he was as he listened to Irene lightly snoring.

Wheels Up Two
September 2037

A few weeks later, after a few more trips, Paul was asked to drive the same tequila van to San Antonio. Once again, he was asked to remain on the Interstate. Paul also suspected he was again tasked with planting high-quality liquor in the enemy's camp, however, no one explicitly told him so. There was also no mention of the Convoy being poised to head over the same route direction later in the evening, but he presumed this was what was planned.

He made it about fifty miles outside of Houston when a motorcycle pulled alongside him and directed him to the side of the road. Paul immediately complied.

The biker, wearing a Department of Energy baseball cap, opened the wooden crates and was not surprised that they were full of tequila. He quickly opened one up and passed it around the group. They all confirmed that the quality was as good as the previous trip.

The biker then asked Paul to follow him back to their camp. Paul did so without any complaint and even assisted them in offloading the boxes. Another biker, wearing a tee shirt with a Department of the Interior logo, demanded that Paul tell him when the Convoy would leave Houston or San Antonio.

After further questioning, Paul confirmed that he thought there was a reasonable chance they'd try to drive a large convoy to San Antonio sometime after midnight. He also assured them that he had not been included in the planning.

This time, they didn't allow Paul to leave with the van. They tied Paul up and threw him in the back of the tent where they had offloaded the liquor.

Paul was questioned several times but lacked information about the convoy plans. Meat, a bald Hispanic-looking biker with a long scar on his face, indicated to Paul that if the Convoy passed this evening, Paul was going to lose an appendage. He'd consider which appendage Paul preferred to lose but would not commit to following his recommendation.

Paul listened as Meat called all the bikers patrolling the Houston to Dallas route and told them to rush to their location between Houston and San Antonio.

While none of the liquor in Paul's tent was supposed to be disturbed, Paul noticed Bikers were entering the tent and walking off with bottles from the already opened wooden crate.

There was no party on track for this evening. From Paul's vantage point, he could tell the bikers were preparing to go to war. They were loading up with weapons and painting their faces with war paint. They revved their bikes up loudly and drove them noisily around the area. It was a fearsome demonstration.

Right before dark, the bikes all left the compound in a noisy rush, no doubt to ambush the Convoy. Paul had no way to communicate with other truckers and feared the worst. He worked to snap the plastic ties they had used to constrain his wrists behind his back but could make no progress against them. His arms were starting to cramp up.

Paul feared that he would be an appendage short by the next day and went over and over in his mind which one he would propose. He ruled out volunteering either of his legs, arms, or penis and was hoping they'd be satisfied with an ear; he had his doubts and couldn't stop dwelling on what Meat would choose to cut off. His undeniable terror was etched on his face, and it seemed to galvanize the bikers that passed through the tent further.

The camp was mostly empty, but he could hear reports over a radio in a nearby tent. A few hours after dark, he overheard a transmission that a convoy was spotted along I-10. Paul feared the worst. He knew the bikers had massed their forces along the expected route and were now in place to snare their prey.

They pulled Paul out of the tent, still strapped to his chair, and let him watch the action from a distance. Paul's dread continued to grow. Gunfire tracers could be seen in the distance. Explosions reverberated up and down the Interstate, and some seemed to shake the ground. With this demonstration of power, Paul was sure that the outlaws would not be content with just an appendage. All Paul could do was pray that his death would come quickly and that someone would get word to Rose and the other members of his family that he was dead.

The noise went on and on. Paul couldn't imagine that the motorcycles could have carried so much ordinance with them. He hoped that some small portion of what he was hearing was being fired by parties friendly to his side.

Paul was moved back into the tent, blindfolded, and gagged. Someone came in and grabbed a few more bottles. He heard bikers mount up and drive off. Paul assumed that the bikers had called for additional assistance to move the captured fuel and other materials obtained from this ambush. Paul remained in the dark for another several hours. He could hear scattered gunfire from time to time. He said as many prayers as possible and soon drifted off to sleep.

The following day, he was awakened roughly by the sound of large vehicles idling nearby. He'd decided that he'd rather lose a foot than an ear; the left one was particularly gimpy, and someday he might be able to afford an artificial one. Ready to announce his decision, the flap to the tent opened, and one of the convoy drivers found him strapped to a heavy safe in the tent. His blindfold and gag were quickly removed, and they cut the ties that had constrained him. The blood surged back into his hands and feet.

"Hokey Pokey, it's you!" The dispatcher that had given him his nickname shouted with excitement. He rushed to Paul and offered him a high five. Paul returned it but desperately needed to relieve himself and rushed out of the tent to a nearby tree before he pissed himself again.

When he returned, his rescuer escorted him to a truck and gave him several bottles of water and candy bars. Paul was famished and polished off these items quickly.

Several vehicles were actually now on site. Two of these were military deuce-and-a-half trucks loaded with policemen in riot gear. The occupants quickly combed the camp for any intelligence related to the motorcycles. They loaded up several boxes of files, computers, and, of course, the crates of tequila.

When they finished their efforts, everyone on site loaded back onto their transport. This small group of vehicles returned to the Interstate and headed back to Houston. Someone else drove the tequila van somewhere. Paul sat in front with the driver.

On the route back to Houston, there was one area where there was considerable evidence that a battle had been fought. There were destroyed motorcycles of all sorts. Some had been blown apart, and others had collided with something unpleasant. There were blood stains on the highway in various locations. However, the bodies of the dead and wounded had already been removed from the scene.

The driver explained as much as he knew to Paul. The previous night, there had been a convoy, but this one was essentially a military operation. The troops had access to night vision equipment that allowed them to see the waiting motorcycles that had arranged themselves along the road, thinking they would control the violence. Suffice it to say they were more than a little surprised by the ferocity and resources that had been concentrated to deal with them. Certain weapons had been deployed that hadn't been used in a decade.

By the time the bikers realized they were in the crosshairs of a well-armed and sizable armed force, they had little chance to react. All most could do was put their bikes into high gear and move in the opposite direction as fast as possible. Some pulled that off, and others were intercepted or ran into trees.

In truth, the battle had not been as decisive as hoped. The commander of the military forces did not have much experience, and he tipped his hand too early. When they encountered the first group of bikers, his forces opened up with too much of a response. An anti-tank weapon can do severe damage to a motorcycle, yet it's noisy, and many other gangs along the route were put on notice that someone had some unusual hardware. This first group was wiped out, but it tipped off the other bikers that something was amiss.

Homeland Security officials had hoped that the slaughter was going to be so devastating that it would end the threat of piracy on the highways. It wasn't clear whether this had been accomplished.

Only a few dozen bikers were killed. Since the police had estimated that more than a hundred bikers were involved in these activities, many were unaccounted for that could still inflict considerable damage on the highways.

From this point forward, there was surprisingly little carnage from the pirates. Many of these bikers had apparently had enough of the mercenary business and were no longer terrorizing the highways. It was an encouraging development.

The news services heard about the conflict, though they had little information about the opposing forces. The lead story on the newswire was that a group of motorcyclists headed for a rally were attacked without explanation by vicious police forces in Texas. The leader of the motorcycle club was not available for comment. Still, the reporter speculated that the elimination of these motorcycles would reduce carbon dioxide emissions.

Guest
October 2037

Paul had been away for several months. Rose and Clare regularly spoke to him on the phone weekly; he drove long trips and had time to chat while driving between major cities.

Rose had her hands full dealing with all the requirements at home and was often exhausted, especially near the end of the day. Sometimes, she had little remaining energy to take Paul's calls and would message him to call back another day.

Rose was the commander and principal worker at the house. She kept the food operations moving but also prepared the kids to defend the property if needed and to be ready for potential emergencies—like the possibility of a hurricane or a tornado. For that, all the young ones were drilled in moving quickly to the root cellar and closing the door on short notice. She also served as a community defense coordinator and met with the neighbors periodically.

Rose had assigned chores to each of the kids, and that helped, but they were often at school. They would catch the bus around seven in the morning and wouldn't get back home until late afternoon. Classes had been arranged so all the kids could ride the same bus.

While the kids were individually tasked, they didn't have much time during the week to complete much of the needed work. Consequently, Rose shouldered most of the tasks. Shortly after the bus pulled off in the morning, Rose would head to the field and do everything required to support the garden before the day got too hot. She battled with weeds, fought insects, and scrounged for fertilizer. Her vegetables demanded more of her time than the children did.

The kids were home over the weekend and assisted by moving harvested vegetables from the field to the barn. They then helped to can or bottle them. Even so, they often seemed to have an excuse to go somewhere. There were birthday parties, the occasional dances, and numerous study groups. One whiff of something happening in the area and one or two of them were gone. Rose didn't have the heart to insist they swear off social opportunities.

When things broke, as they did with some regularity, Jose tried to step in and solve the issue with mixed success. Paul had spent some time with Jose, coaching him on adjusting the prices on the various fuses to defend them from exorbitant electrical spot prices. Jose was a fast learner and monitored their electricity usage.

In addition, Jose was tasked with keeping the septic tank system operating, monitoring the water pump, and managing any cottage maintenance issues. Some of these tasks were clearly out of his league. There were weekends when he'd start a repair job on Friday afternoon and then wrap it up or abandon it before he went to bed Sunday night. He also chopped wood, coordinated the compost, and still found time for high school dates.

Marie was tagged with managing the chickens. She had to feed them and clean out their roosts daily, gather their eggs, and identify any predators. The significant threats came from snakes, raccoons, and wild dogs. Others were available to deal with these animals when they appeared.

Claire's job was now meal management. She was responsible for making breakfast and making the sandwiches for lunch. Clare was also the supervisor for canning operations. Her job was to boil and clean the jars, fill, seal, and store them. It was essential to follow a "first in, last out" approach so that the content of the older jars was eaten before they expired. Collectively, they ate so much that it wasn't usually an issue.

Della managed the laundry. She combined everyone's dirty clothes into large washing loads, as electricity prices allowed, and hung them on the line to dry. She was also expected to keep a close eye on the weather so that she could bring the dry clothes in before the next rains soaked them. She also monitored everyone else and their chores and stepped in where needed.

Running a low-tech agriculture operation was labor-intensive and incredibly demanding. Despite this, Jose and his sisters had never felt more needed and loved than they were now in their current situation.

Clare had regular hot flashes, and her only defense in the summer was to reduce her clothing layers. In fact, she regularly wore a bra and panties around the house or a bathing suit. Jose never complained, and Rose felt too guilty about the limited electricity situation to compel her to wear more.

One fall Saturday, Rose smelled something cooking and wandered into the kitchen. Clare was in the final stages of preparing dinner and had made an effort to dress well for the occasion; the outfit she had chosen was a tight fit in her condition, but looked presentable, despite the beads of sweat running down her neck and onto her dress.

Claire had gone to considerable trouble with this meal. She had plucked and roasted a chicken in the electric oven; this would be the first meat they had seen at home in several weeks. Jose and Marie sat in the living room soaking in the aroma of dinner, and Rose sat down with them. Scanning the room, she noticed someone had set an extra plate on the table.

There was a knock at the door. Della, conveniently standing next to the front door, opened it. She said nothing and gestured for someone to enter.

Rose was surprised that Della knew their visitor. The young man was attractive, at least a decade older, and dressed in worn coveralls. Her immediate guess was that this gentleman was courting Della.

Jose stood up, approached him to shake his hand, and greeted him. "Mr. Hatfield, good to see you, sir. Have you met Clare's Mother, Rose?"

"I have not," he said. "Ma'am, my name is Johnse Hatfield." I'm the home economics teacher at the local High School."

Clare momentarily came out of the kitchen, and from the intimate glance that the two shared, Rose surmised that she wasn't just his student.

"Just call me Rose. What brings you to our house tonight?" It came across as an inquisition; Rose was prepared to probe hard to learn why this young man was somehow connected to her daughter.

Johnse seemed taken back by the intensity of her interest. "I'm sorry; I thought Clare told you she invited me to dinner. Please forgive me for the interruption. Should I come back another time?"

"No, please have a seat," Rose said as Clare waited for them to sit together across from each other in the living room. She then returned to the kitchen to continue making dinner. Jose, Della, and even little Marie had all taken their places at the table and were fiddling with the silverware and napkins. They all had one ear tuned to the conversation.

"Nice place you have here."

"It's a bit more crowded than it used to be."

"It was awfully kind of you to invite these three young ones to join your family," he motioned to the dining room. "I've had Della and Jose in class; I assure you, they are serious and capable students. It shouldn't take them long to catch up with their classmates."

"Well, they've all been a welcome addition to our family," Rose responded to his small talk but was not going to let her original question go unanswered. "What brings you to our neck of the woods this evening?"

"Has Clare mentioned anything about me?"

"My Clare? She's also one of your students?"

"Rose, how soon do you think dinner will be ready? Do we have a few minutes to step outside? Please allow me to respond to your question properly."

Jose, Della, and Marie all filed from the table into the kitchen to join Clare.

"Yes, we have time, especially if the answer is complicated." Rose motioned to the front door, and Johnse led the way to the porch. Rose then directed him to walk back towards the garden area.

"Lovely property," Johnse said along the way.

Rose ignored his observation. "Perhaps now you can explain why my question was one you wanted to answer privately?"

"It's a simple answer. I'm in love with your daughter."

"My daughter is fifteen, you're what, forty?"

"I'm sorry. I'm twenty-six. An eleven-year difference is not that large an age difference for a couple."

"Does the term statutory rape mean anything to you?"

"These are strange times. You're referencing a term from a different world. Clare is the most mature woman I've ever met. We're meant to be together."

"The kid's an awkward teenager!"

"An amazing one."

"Are you the father of her baby?"

"Yes."

Rose let that thought sink in as they continued walking toward the fields. The idea of a teacher in authority having unprotected sex with their young daughter set her on edge. There was nothing he could say that was going to fix this ethical breach. She visualized herself finding the principal at the High School on Monday and sharing this confession with him. No doubt they would send him packing later that day.

"So, why are you here?" Rose hissed.

"I want to ask for her hand in marriage. I'd have asked her father, but I understand he's on the road."

"Are you shitting me?" Rose said, a little tightly wired. "You knock up one of your students and then have the balls to come to her house to ask one of her parents if you can marry her? She's just a child."

"Now you're the one who's missed the big picture. Clare has been working hard with you for years. From what she's told me, it sounds like she never had a childhood. I love her and want to raise our child with her. How can I get you to accept that?"

"What will you do to make a living? Surely the school won't let you continue teaching classes after *this*?"

"Look, I come from a long line of moonshiners. From a young age, I've learned to distill alcohol so pure and strong that you can drink it or use it to fuel your vehicle."

"This just keeps getting better. How do you make money doing that?"

"We own an alcohol distillery business. It's time for me to return home to take it over."

"And what about my daughter? How does she fit in your future?"

"I can homeschool her for the rest of her high school education. She can later attend college in her spare time. She'll now have a business management role in the company and be a full-time mom. We'll make it work."

"This is all new information."

"Yes, but it's moving forward. I've given my final teaching notice and will finish in December."

"So, you want to marry my baby and quit your job around the same time?"

"I'm afraid those two events are inseparable. I had to decide between teaching and your daughter. Her pregnancy has moved up the timeline, but not my intentions. I'll make her happy."

"Where is home?"

"Ever heard of Pikeville, Kentucky? It's not far from the West Virginia border."

"Look, this is a lot for me to process. I'm going to need to update her father.'

"Of course."

Rose thought a bit. "Why would you choose someone so young and innocent? Surely you must have had a lot of other prospects in college?"

"When I first met Clare, I thought she was a timid young student. At first, it was a struggle to convince her to talk in class."

"That sounds like my daughter."

"Ah, but that's where you're wrong. As we got to know each other, she took me to places I didn't even know existed."

"You mean in the woods?"

"No, I mean emotionally. Our chemistry was so strong, we just gave in?"

"Look, we don't need to explore this any further today. You're both too young, but at least you've got a plan to make ends meet." She quickly decided that the trip to the principal's office was off the table, at least for the next few days.

"I'll take that as a 'yes,'" Johnse said.

"I'll support whatever Clare wants to do. I never thought I'd lose her to a suitor at this age."

"You're not losing her. You're gaining a grandchild and a son-in-law."

"That's up to Clare. I'm guessing that you haven't asked her yet?"

"She's already agreed but insisted you guys be on board."

"Fifteen years ago, I'd have already called the police."

"Fifteen years ago, they would have come."

He was smart, savvy, and good-looking. She wasn't sure if he was really crazy about their daughter or simply doing the honorable thing. She was startled when she realized Clare would have wanted him either way. He could offer her a better future than the more limited one she had previously fretted about. Maybe it wasn't his fault that their birth control method hadn't worked?

Rose had already decided to allow him to marry their daughter but would not share that information with him today. She was sure she needed to take some time to consider his proposal; otherwise, he might second-guess the deal if Clare's parents relented too quickly.

Johnse offered Rose his hand to escort her back to the cabin.

She didn't take it but didn't slap it away either. The two of them returned to the cabin, both deep in thought.

***

Irene heard the doorbell and went to answer it. An attractive woman about her age stared back at her. "Can I help you?"

"Yes, I'm looking for my husband."

"I'm sorry, but you must have the wrong address," Irene said dismissively, closing the door. The visitor pressed back on the door before she could close it.

"His name is Eacher." Jasmine quickly added and restored the door to the fully open position. "I think you know him."

Irene felt like she'd just been hit by a large stick. Eacher had mentioned that he had previously been married, but she never presumed that he still was. "Who are you?"

"My name is Jasmine. Eacher didn't mention that he was paying me to live in a hotel down the street?"

"No, he didn't. How long have you been living there?"

"Not long. I came here to surprise him. I had been living at our farm in Arkansas."

Irene was emotionally reeling. She had not expected that Eacher might still be legally married. This woman wore a wedding ring on her left hand. Irene stood there with the door wide open.

"Do you mind if I come in?" She pushed past Irene and walked into the living room without waiting for a response. She quickly scanned the furniture and the artwork on the walls.

"What do you think you're doing?" Irene asked.

"Perhaps I'm the one that should be asking that question. It appears that you're living with my husband."

"Yes, we're sharing this place."

"Then which room is yours?" Jasmine asked in what sounded like her official capacity as wife.

"It's the master bedroom."

"Well, mind if I take a look?" She quickly turned and walked toward the back of the apartment. "There's only one bedroom?"

"Yes, we share it."

"You're sharing a bedroom with my spouse?"

Irene turned red. She pulled out her phone and called Eacher. "Eacher, your wife is here."

"She is?"

That settled it. Irene hung up immediately. The phone screen lit up, showing that Eacher was trying to call back, but Irene had turned the ring volume off. She stuck the phone in her pocket as it continued to vibrate.

"What's going on here?" Irene asked.

"I'm the wife; I think I'm entitled to ask questions. How soon can you clear out of this apartment?"

"I'll need a few days."

"Well, in that case, just let him know I'm heading back to our hotel room." Jasmine abruptly turned around and quickly walked out the door.

When Eacher arrived at the apartment fifteen minutes later, he unlocked the door lock and the deadbolt. He pried the door open as far as the security clasp would allow. "Irene, we need to talk," Eacher called out from the front door.

"You think?"

"I can explain."

"You can explain why you never told me you were still married or why your wife was staying in a hotel room not far from our apartment that you're paying for?"

"Yeah, that. I thought she would stay at my farm for the winter."

"You let your wife stay at your farm alone? You never mentioned that."

"A glass vase shattered next to where he was trying to poke his head through the door."

"Please let me in, I can explain."

"The hell you can. I thought I could trust you."

"You can."

"And this is what trust looks like?"

"No, I'm sorry, I should have told you sooner."

"You got that right. Do you need anything out of the apartment?"

"What, you're kicking me out?"

"I don't date married men."

"Me either." Eacher quipped immediately.

This remark surprised her, and she couldn't help but laugh. She walked to the door, pushed it forward, and released the security clasp. She then twisted the knob and opened the door slightly.

The door slowly opened, and Eacher stuck his head around the corner. He was still wary of flying objects. "Mind if I come in?"

"No, but you should leave the door open in case your wife comes by and catches us together."

Eacher closed and locked the door behind him and turned and faced her.

"So, you've met Jasmine? Sounds like a rough introduction."

"Nah, she met me. She stopped by to give me the full treatment."

"Unbelievable!" Eacher said. "I hadn't seen that woman in over twenty years when she called me and begged for assistance. I let her stay at my farm, partly to help her and mostly to keep her at some distance."

"Nice guy."

"Not really."

"Apparently, she's still your wife?" Irene looked at Eacher to ascertain his reaction.

"That's only because she regularly refused to execute the paperwork I mailed her. She left me and then wouldn't give me legal satisfaction by making it official."

"Nice lady."

"I'll say. She was set up to spend the winter on my farm and showed up here without warning."

"So, you've seen her since she arrived in town?"

"Afraid so. She called me from a local restaurant to let me know she was here."

"Have you asked her to sign the divorce paperwork?"

"No, I'd have to recreate those documents. I didn't bring them with me from home."

"She was ballsy to come here to our apartment to introduce herself."

"Seems so."

"She demanded to see our bedroom and was wearing a wedding ring."

"No good deed goes unpunished."

"Now what?"

"I don't know. What do you think she wants?"

"Not me. Jasmine made that clear a long time ago."

"Then what?"

"Some type of improvement from her current living situation? She wants access to the money I'm getting paid by the government?"

"Can't you just give her money?"

"I have been. I guess it's not enough, even though it's draining my savings." Eacher said. "She's old and destitute."

"And she'd put up with you to improve her financial security?"

"I'm not sure she's thought this through. She did a pretty good job of pissing you off." Eacher chuckled. "Perhaps she thought that would send you packing."

"I pretended it did. We both know that this apartment is leased in my name."

"Did you tell her that?"

"And ruin her bluff? Not a chance!"

"So now what?"

"Not sure. Let's sleep on it and talk about it over the next few days."

"You still plan on paying her hotel bills?"

"I don't think I have a choice. But I can't do it for much longer."

The Ellen Show
November 2037

Today's Heroes interviewed former President Ellen Winthrop on national television. Dressed in a worn pair of overalls with a pressed white tee shirt beneath, her hair and makeup were professionally coifed. The camera panned a small farming operation in northern Florida from a perspective slightly above the roof of a small log cabin on the property.

The weather was warm, and the fields were meticulously cleared and raked.

She approached a fruit tree, reached up, and pulled a beautifully polished grapefruit from one of the branches. It was not clear whether she actually picked it off the tree or simply retrieved it from a location where it had been placed. It looked like it had been polished.

"Tell me, do you spend much time on farms or orchards?" Ricard Millont, a regular celebrity interviewer and the most well-known member of the show asked her.

"Every chance I get!" Ellen enthusiastically responded, though the skin on her hands and face was curiously pale and showed little evidence of spending much time in the sun.

"You were interested in sharing your take on why our country's deurbanization project is vitally important to our nation."

"It's important for our national leaders to explain our reasoning. Given my recent sabbatical from office, I'm enjoying life with fewer distractions than I'd normally have to deal with. I can't think of anything I'd rather do than talk about living in the country on this wonderful property."

"Well, that's dedication," Ricard said. "Please go ahead."

"First of all, let me point out that I'm not the one that started this evolution. It's been happening for more than twenty years. When numerous workers determined they could live anywhere and interact with other workers through various software applications, hybrid jobs became popular."

'So you think the germ of the idea was technology?"

"That was part of it. The convenience of remote networking, the high cost of housing, and local taxes in certain parts of the country really introduced many people to living outside the major cities."

"How have things changed since?"

"We've made a lot of progress."

"How so."

"We've transformed our lives."

"Was that driven by Net Zero?"

"Much of it was. As hydrocarbons inevitably soared in price, our previous lifestyle failed on numerous levels. Transportation fuel was too expensive, and the McMansions were too distant and large for most families to heat, cool, or maintain. Essentially, the suburbs were cut off from the cities and evolved into collections of small farms."

"Which was important because food became scarce."

"Exactly. Many people were also attracted to the opportunity to reduce their energy footprint and provide for their own sustenance."

"So, the enthusiasm for these more sustainable lifestyles really drove the deurbanization?"

"Partly. It also took a lot of Presidential leadership. My predecessor recognized that the evolution to small, labor-intensive farms was the most practical vision for the future. It's a huge challenge to get enough electricity for everyone from wind and solar power; fossil fuels are finite and won't last much longer, and many people are rightfully afraid of nuclear bombs, I mean nuclear energy. We can no longer support a world of unbridled consumption."

"So deurbanization is a step in the right direction."

"It's a better lifestyle that we should all embrace."

"You've not mentioned anything about climate change."

"No need to. We all understand that our civilization has no choice. We have to dial down our individual energy consumption or extreme weather events will make us miserable."

"That's not the direction President Almond is taking our country."

"No, it's not, but it ought to be. Our planet seems assured of reaching a global population of ten billion people by the end of this century." With these remarks, Ellen looked far into the distance and then turned back to look directly into the camera. "We can no longer support the level of materialism that we all became accustomed to. The real beauty is that if we each discipline ourselves to only use a minor amount of energy, our country is no longer part of the global problem. Confident in the worthiness of our lifestyles, we can sit back and wait for the rest of the world to follow our lead."

"So, you're asking people to continue to whittle down their energy utilization?"

"No one will prevent them from doing so, but that approach alone probably won't be enough. If the government hadn't taken action to make energy expensive, people would foolishly choose to use too much. Also, why should wealthy people be entitled to use more energy than the rest of us? We should limit their usage, too. The government really does know what's best for our country."

"You mean our current administration?"

"No, of course not. Wild West Jenny is dazed and confused. Her willingness to distribute guns and ammunition through the Post Office has led to a lot of senseless violence. Her attack on that motorcycle club in Texas was reprehensible. She thinks we can all go back to using fossil fuels and forget about our personal carbon footprints. I don't believe many voters will follow her lead."

The discussion continued along this path for another ten minutes. The show ended with a scene of Ellen riding an electric scooter around the property and waving at the camera.

***

"Are you ready to move into *our* apartment?" Eacher asked Jasmine over the phone.

"Sure, how soon can you pick me up?" She purred.

"I could be there in about twenty minutes."

"I'll be ready."

Eacher hung up and scanned the apartment. It was large enough for three people, though it only one bathroom. He didn't mention to Jasmine that Irene still lived there.

Eacher couldn't believe that Irene was the one who suggested that she move in. He'd have never had the audacity to propose it to her. However, she smartly figured out that it was the most practical way to go with money still tight and utilities expensive. In addition, the economy was still challenged and jobs were scarce. None of them had ever had any kids, so there weren't likely to be other family members petitioning for a place to crash. Irene and Eacher worked long hours at the office, so there would be advantages to having someone at home if any prowlers took an interest in their apartment complex.

An important question was whether she would put up a fight or accept the proposed arrangement; she didn't seem to have any other compelling options.

A second concern was whether she could get along with Irene. Eacher had heard that one word for trouble in Chinese included a character that depicted two women under one roof.

The proposed offer was logical. Jasmine could live here and sleep on the couch. She could have the entry closet for her stuff. In addition, she'd need to keep the place clean, do the laundry, and prepare the meals. If she could secure an outside job, they could renegotiate the expenses and the chores.

Neither Irene nor Eacher were sure this was the right plan, but it was rational and kind. If she wanted to live on the street without resources, it'd be her doing. They both understood that this was an offer she couldn't refuse.

When he brought Jasmine back, he walked her in the door, sat her on the couch, and explained the arrangement. Her face fell, but she did not turn it down or complain too loudly. He carried her suitcase to their entry closet to seal the deal. She allowed it to stay there and headed into the kitchen to make dinner.

Frankenfleet
December 2037

With harvest over, there was little to do outside other than rake up the fields and move anything that wasn't dirt into a compost pile.

Paul was returning back home for the first time in five months. He had used some of his earnings to rent a small used motorcycle. Over the last few months, he had seen very few highway vehicles. Now that most of the fields were cleared, he was greatly surprised by the number and condition of cars on the roads. It was something out of a Mad Max movie.

Most single-person vehicles were electric battery-operated scooters or fuel-efficient motorcycles like the one that Paul was driving.

There were a few different groupings of multi-passenger rides. Almost ten years earlier, most people had sold their vehicles to buyers who lived in other countries. The ones that didn't attract an offer were mainly worn out or busted. A few wealthy people kept them hoping fuel costs would come down, but that rarely happened until recently.

The largest group now on the road was gasoline or diesel-fueled. Almost all of these were in rough shape, and the people attempting to drive them were likely out joyriding. These vehicles were mainly rusty orange, and the metal panels were full of rust holes or patched with duct tape or fiberglass.

A small subset of cars and trucks looked very similar to the first group. Still, it featured scuba tanks or other gas tanks – usually mounted on racks above the trunk or roof or stacked in the bed of pickup trucks. These were operating on natural gas or propane. In general, these vehicles were in a little better condition. They might get regular use if the drivers had access to fuel. Operating these vehicles with natural gas was perhaps a third of the fuel cost of operating them with gasoline or diesel.

Then there was the category of "everything else." These included bicycles, horses pulling carts or trailers, and almost everything you could imagine. Some Chinese-built electric vehicles were newer and not bad-looking. These cars would be less expensive to operate than most combustion engines – if only electricity prices were lower.

Paul was surprised to see a few luxury electric SUVs. He did his best to discern the age and dress of any occupants so he could speculate on their story. Most were older vehicles that likely dated back to when the government mainly gave wealthy people subsidies to buy such cars to signal virtue. For the most part, the only access to spare parts came from junkyards. After US auto manufacturers had tanked, it was difficult to get spare parts. Missing hoods, bent quarter panels, and wood bumpers were standard. What aesthetic component couldn't be replaced was skipped or crafted in the garage or wood shed.

Even so, there was a confident, outgoing attitude this winter that had not been evidenced in recent years. People were getting out of the house and making trips or at least testing their transportation. The whole exercise might be over by the time planting began, but it filled him with confidence that people were itching to get back on the road.

Paul pulled into his driveway. There was a flurry of activity in the yard. Jose was heating water on the back porch grill. Della was bringing in fresh sheets from the line. Rose was moving a mattress into the garage. Clare was nowhere in sight, but a young man was standing outside.

"You must be Johnse," Paul said.

"Yes, and you are..." Johnse stopped for a second to look him over.

"Paul, I'm Clare's dad."

"Of course. The economist truck driver. I've heard you used to teach at the local college."

"Yep, true. Why is everyone moving around so quickly?"

"Clare is in labor. She wanted to have the baby in the barn so she didn't make too much of a mess in the house."

"Yes, but is that a sterile environment?"

Johnse pulled a small flask out of his pocket. "Here, taste this."

Paul took a swig. "Woah, is that strong! Is that rubbing alcohol?"

"Moonshine. It's a homemade batch I made with my portable still. We're using it to sterilize all the surfaces in our makeshift delivery room."

"That will keep the germs out!"

"Do you know anything about birthing?"

"Just enough to know not to get in Rose's way. How far is she along?"

"About seven centimeters at the moment," Johnse said.

"Today's the day!" Paul said excitedly. "So glad I could be here!"

Johnse headed to the back porch, and Paul walked through the barn's side door. The mattress had been set up in the area that had once been the harness room. The room was comfortably warm. He spotted Clare and Rose together on the ground. "How are you?"

"Welcome home, you're just in time," Rose said.

'Hi, Dad," Clare said.

"I didn't think you were due for another week," Paul said, looking the room up and down.

"Can't say 'no' to this baby!" Clare closed her eyes as a mild contraction came and went.

Cappy was curled up next to her, wanting to be in the action. When he saw Paul, he stood up and walked toward him, wagging his tail. Paul scratched him behind the ears.

Johnse walked into the room carrying a pot of boiling water. Della followed with clean towels, and Marie came in with flowers.

"It's getting crowded in here," Paul observed amidst all the activity underway.

"It's still not time," Rose said. "I bet we have a few more hours before she's ready to push."

"Why don't you and Paul catch up with each other?" Johnse said. I know you haven't seen each other in a while. Clare and I just want to spend more time practicing her breathing exercises."

"It's a little late to rehearse those. You'll need to go with what you've worked on." Rose said, but took his advice and left them with the other children as she and Paul wandered outside.

"Any questions?"

"I'd be more comfortable if you had some professional help."

"Our midwife stopped by this morning and asked us to call her when Clare dilated to eight centimeters. She only lives about a mile away."

"It's hard to believe our little girl is about to have a baby. Still no idea what sex it will be?"

"Based on how Clare carried the baby, the midwife is convinced it will be a little girl."

"Quite a prediction when we've never had an ultrasound or fetal monitor."

"We've recently visited the doctor at the free clinic. He was confident that the baby was not in a breach position. He didn't seem particularly worried about the difficulty of this labor. Clare is so young and strong; she's much less likely to have delivery issues than if she were twenty years older."

"She's gotten all the proper vitamins and supplements?" Paul asked.

"Yes, the free clinic loaded us up," Rose said.

"And, this guy Johnse. Do you really think he's on the level? I was certain that the sperm donor was a lot younger. You know, someone closer to her age. What a mistake for a teacher to make!"

"You mean getting a student pregnant or not practicing more effective birth control?"

"Both," Paul said.

"Yeah, it does make me question his judgment. They're moving shortly."

"How are they going to travel?" Paul asked.

"I'm not sure about that part. Ask Johnse."

Later in the evening, the baby boy arrived without a hitch. Clare was moved back into her bedroom, and she and Johnse used a dresser drawer as a bassinet.

***

A few weeks later, Johnse and Clare were ready to move to Pikeville. His mother had a room for both of them in her home, and she was sending a delivery vehicle to pick them up.

The truck arrived a few days later. The driver was an older employee with lots of alcohol to deliver. He had apparently made some distribution stops along the way.

Claire had packed her few possessions, and Rose had packed a trunk for a few more items Rose thought she would need.

There were tears all around as the truck pulled onto the highway. Clare was nursing the baby in the middle of the seat, and Johnse sat beside her next to the window. Just like that, they were gone.

Rose and Paul stood frozen on the gravel in the driveway, watching the truck leave. Their three new family members and Cappy stood next to them.

There was nothing to be sad about. Clare was hitched to what seemed like a solid young man. She was too young to be married by their expectations but less so by the standards of the area she was moving to. It looked like Clare was about to become hillbilly royalty!

***

Eacher, Irene, and Jasmine had been living together for about a month, and the holidays were upon them.

Jasmine had not been able to secure a job, so she was still on the hook for most chores. As it turned out, she was a pretty capable cook. This revelation surprised Irene the most, since Eacher never previously mentioned that Jasmine had culinary skills. Perhaps Jasmine's meal preparation had improved because her efforts were now subject to the scrutiny of another woman, but in time she realized that the problem was probably with Eacher's memory.

Irene occasionally probed Jasmine's recollection of events while she was married to Eacher. One evening during dinner she prompted her by asking, "What was your favorite vacation?"

"I'd say it was the time we went to Niagara Falls." Jasmine responded with no hesitation. "We stayed in a high-rise Marriot hotel with a room that overlooked Niagara Falls State Park. We were so close to the top of the falls that we could hear a continuous roar. We had breakfast in our room and I still remember the Eggs Benedict. We hiked the first day and the next morning, we stood on the deck of a tour boat that took us right into the mist of the lower river."

"Eacher, any of that ring a bell?" Irene teased him.

"I'm sorry, what year was that?" Eacher asked.

"It was our Second Anniversary and we took a side trip from one of your geological conferences in Buffalo." Jasmine added.

"Yeah, that sounds right," Eacher said.

Irene mercifully stopped pressing him for details. She speculated whether he had deliberately suppressed certain memories from the trauma of his previous relationship or if his brain just wasn't wired to store such observations. The latter theory seemed more probable.

Irene's attention to detail was also somewhat exacting. The household budget had twenty-five different categories and she required Jasmine to stay within these limits. In addition, Jasmine needed to produce every receipt before Irene would provide her more money. This exchange got a little testy at times, but the two of them made it work.

As the holidays approached, Irene would not authorize any money for decorations or gifts. Jasmine bristled from this particular constraint and insisted that it was important for them to celebrate the season; she spent a lot of time making ornaments, threading popcorn strings, and constructing a holiday reef from some pine trees nearby. Irene appreciated her efforts to make the house more festive, but Eacher never seemed to notice.

Eacher was an old dog that fell asleep watching television on the sofa after dinner and got up to go to the bathroom numerous times each night. His hearing was not good and often needed others to repeat what they had just said. Irene wasn't worried that Jasmine would fight to get him back.

Jasmine continued to seek employment in her spare time but was unable to secure a position. Eacher and Irene encouraged her, yet also wanted to keep her expectations low.

While the three of them in tight quarters could have been an awkward situation, it wasn't. Out of consideration, Irene and Eacher rarely showed affection towards each other in Jasmine's presence. Also, Irene did her best to make her feel welcome and appreciated.

There were sitcoms on television of groups of older men and women living together to shepherd their limited resources. The three of them occasionally watched one of these shows on television and it always prompted a lot of laughter.

Changes
January 2038

The restoration of the food kitchens resulted in a stalemate that kept large numbers of primarily idle homeless people near the center of town. Any townhouses or homes where street people squatted essentially trashed the surrounding neighborhoods. Many of the owners preferred to abandon their properties rather than put their lives at risk.

When Marco first noticed that the headcount for free meals was shrinking, he made it his business to discover why. If their facility lost too many participants, there was a good chance it would merge with another.

Marco's first hypothesis was that people were dying. It was a cold time of year, and hypothermia could quickly kill anyone exposed. However, when he visited the morgue at the hospital, it gave him no evidence for that conclusion.

He walked the streets looking for an answer. A moving truck was parked in front of one of the properties previously occupied by squatters. To his surprise, several people were moving furniture into the building. He followed them inside. The lights evidenced that someone had turned on the utilities, a rare development in this part of town. A young woman directed the movers where to place the sofa they had just carried in.

After the workers deposited it where she directed, they returned to the truck. He welcomed her to the neighborhood and asked if he could assist.

"Not now," she said. "I need to make sure my furniture makes it into my home."

"Of course," he said. "Are you new to Houston?"

"Yes," she said as she directed the next load of furniture into a bedroom.

"That's nice. Where are you coming from?"

"Pittsburgh," she said. "I just took a geologist job in downtown Houston. It's hard to believe that this townhouse was so affordable."

The movers came in again and were setting an easy boy chair in the living room. She placed it near the sofa and oriented it to face a wall where Marco imagined she'd hang a large-screen television.

"This place looks great! Did you restore it yourself?"

"Oh no, I have no time for that. I bought it through a multiple listing service here in Houston based on the pictures online." The movers came in and placed her washer and dryer in a utility room, and she watched them like a hawk as they installed the hoses and tightened all the connections.

"That's interesting," Marco said.

"Really, how so?" she asked.

"I never noticed before how nice this neighborhood is." Marco didn't want to apprise her that this area had been a bit of a war zone a year earlier.

"Even so, I did buy the security package, you know. Just to be safe."

"The security package?"

"Yes, that gives me some electronic monitoring protection and security patrols that can be immediately dispatched to my location if there are any issues. I insisted on that when I noticed another unit on this street had boarded windows."

"Oh, that's right." Marco agreed but was surprised that it was only one. He walked to the window, looked out, and confirmed her count.

The movers came through again; this time, they had wardrobe boxes that she directed into her walk-in closet.

"Look, I really need to focus on ensuring that everything I put on the moving truck gets offloaded. Thanks for stopping by."

"Well, I'd do the same thing," Marco said as he left her space and looked at the other properties on her street. The entire block had been cleaned up. That meant that not only were cleaning services and repair services utilized to restore everything to higher standards but that others had already moved in. He'd also recognized one of the workers as someone who no longer ate at the dining hall. Jobs were busting out all over. Security, maintenance, repair, cleaning, moving, and food delivery. Employed people could afford to pay for their own apartments, food, and privacy.

Marco was inspired. Money was flowing through some of the streets of this town again. Neighborhoods that people had given up on were improving. Two blocks over, he noticed that the refurbishment operations were just getting started.

Squatters were being ejected from units, and their few possessions were dumped in the streets. Transients and squatters were forced from blocks, along with the cockroaches and rats that were driven out by pesticides. Police officers enforced the evictions and ensured that the displaced occupants didn't do any further damage as they left the area. If it was a brisk day, they might transport them to a shelter far from the property where they had been evicted.

Handymen were working on various exterior items – mainly removing boarded windows, replacing glass, and painting the exterior. There was a lot of activity in motion. He asked one of the painters who was in charge. They pointed toward a model unit on the corner.

He knocked on the door. It opened, and a muscular-looking foreman stood in front of him. He recognized him from the meal center. "Pablo, do you need any help with this work?"

"I remember you. You're that little guy that burned down the soup kitchen."

"Of course, you know me. We go way back."

"That was you, right?"

"Yeah, but I was just following orders." Marco tried to distance himself from his notoriety. He was prepared to simply leave once he had been recognized.

"I could use someone willing to follow my direction. What do you know about the repair business?" The foreman looked stressed.

"Getting replacement parts and finishes is the hardest part."

"You're right about that. Do you think you could help locate those items?"

"Of course," Marco quickly responded. He had little idea what Pablo wanted, yet he was sure he could do anything that anyone in this area could do.

"Okay, start tomorrow and wear some old clothes. See you at 8 o'clock right here."

"See you then."

Marco took the rest of the afternoon to do some research. He went to the city library and learned what he could about the current real estate market. Prices had been in a slump for a long time, though they were recently showing movement. Maybe it was a dead cat bounce, but he wanted to be part of it.

The next day, he showed up and was asked to compile a list of everything needed to restore the properties they were working on. He went door to door and composed a list. He tried to describe things as simply as possible. Glass panes, steel rails, and door knobs. He asked the foreman where he needed to go to get these items, but the foreman had no suggestions. The box stores had folded years earlier, and every item required finding a source that already had them in inventory.

The foreman gave him a credit card and an electric scooter, and he looked for everything he needed. It was a slow and inefficient process, but it gave him a reason to interact with many businesses. A few items needed were lifted from an apartment in another neighborhood occupied by squatters who were pretty unconcerned when he walked out with them. By the end of the week, he had almost everything required for the complex, and the foreman had moved him to a different project.

Within a month, Marco had graduated from an expediter role to a property agent. He learned how to identify properties their Chinese investor could acquire that had a high probability of success. He also figured out how to research property titles and assess the amount of effort required to update them, as well as how to estimate the potential return from the investment. Having expanded his focus from residential to commercial and even manufacturing, he went from being paid by the hour to being paid as a share of profits.

Lawyers were needed to unscrew the property titles where the original owners could no longer be located, and he also got a referral fee when he selected which ones to use.

He flipped a few projects, which gave him some capital. He discovered that many of the patrons of the soup kitchens were ready to take on jobs and improve their personal situations.

He used his capital to set up a maid service, an apartment refurbishment business, and an employee recruiting business. Although wages were low for everyone, he made a share of the profits from everyone he employed.

Marco ate at the free meal centers at times, but only when he was recruiting staff. He often invited his newest workers to stop by his apartment to note how well he was living; he wanted them to believe that success was possible.

Inspired workers tend to be hard workers, and for them to learn that it was possible to use the refrigerator and fill it with food was about the most powerful thing that he was capable of sharing with them. He felt at home for the first time in years.

Yet, while he fed them the dream of using their appliances, he had no expectations that most of his workers would ever reach it. Many jobs are compensated based on the general level of affluence of the society in which they operate. The work required to give a two yuan haircut in a poor country might differ slightly from that needed for a five hundred yuan trim in a wealthy nation. Most workers were barely getting by on the wages available. The United States was a long way from returning the masses to higher levels of prosperity.

***

Two decades earlier, the top ten percent of wage earners accounted for half the country's income and three-quarters of the country's taxes. Many of these ten percenters had gone along with policies that had inflicted considerable damage on the economy.

Yet, when things got ugly, many simply took their skills and assets and replanted them outside the United States. Even the few that elected to stay redirected their investments into companies that focused their operations overseas. Private investment in the United States had effectively ceased.

Jenny was sure that the cities would need to lead the nation's recovery. Some, like Houston, seemed to be starting to move in the right direction. Most, however, were still struggling with the fundamentals.

Public officials deliberately inculcated a fear of starvation in the majority of the country as part of their de-growth strategy. The previous administrations wanted people to leave the cities and grow their own food.

That unplugged lifestyle fit Ellen's notion of what a sustainable society should look like. She attracted bureaucrats who set low limits on the rights of others. How many people should be allowed to have a personal vehicle? How many square feet of housing should be permitted per individual? Who should be allowed to take trips on airplanes? They spoke of capitalism but really aimed at "equality of outcomes." It sounded scientific and fair but was neither. It just left most people poorer and doubting their ability to benefit from their efforts.

The electrical grid needed to be more reliable. Many fossil fuel plants that had been closed had since been gutted or sabotaged. A few had returned online, but electricity demand was still too weak to persuade investors to build more power plants. With few exceptions, residents were still either too afraid or too resource-challenged to utilize much electricity.

It didn't help that the national electrical grid was now compartmentalized into thirty different, mostly unconnected entities. The good news was that if the local electrical grid crashed, the other systems had little domino effect; any single grid that had to be shut down temporarily could be restarted much sooner.

However, the new changes left some areas with higher service levels than others. Some systems, like the one that supported the nation's capital, were more extensive and well supported by federal government assistance. Others provided little electricity, even for those who could afford it.

Most emerging companies needed more electricity to operate their businesses. They could sometimes help themselves by buying natural gas electricity generators for backup, but that only worked if the local natural gas network had sufficient capacity.

Companies also had to guess whether sufficient demand for their services or products would exist. Most people were poor and had few resources to buy anything.

Businesses in the United States also faced country risks. If she loses the national election, even solid companies will be in trouble. Few were willing to bet on her continuation in office, and a nascent recovery coughed and sputtered.

Midterms were only ten months away and would challenge Jenny's team. A few things were moving in the right direction, but much too slowly. The rest of the economy was either stalled or moving backward. Real improvement would take time.

View from the Top
March 2038

Jenny had been scanning the media and watching television broadcasts. They urgently pleaded for the country to persist with its Net Zero efforts.

Extreme weather events were featured around the clock; the international networks could often milk a single hurricane for several weeks of coverage. When live extreme weather events weren't available, they had a series of greatest weather disasters that filled in the gaps. It was weather porn and it was continually aired to suggest that the weather was more extreme or unusual than it had been in the past. The statistics confirmed that extreme weather events were not more frequent or more intense. However, that perspective was not shared broadly.

When Jenny bemoaned this persistent weather horror fixation, Eacher and Irene reminded her of their access to Windy in China.

Jenny asked that they travel to China to get a first-hand perspective on what was going on with the global climate. That information would give her a useful perspective on the veracity of the transmitted content aimed at the general public.

A government travel agency procured plane tickets on an Air China flight, and they flew to Beijing.

***

Windy met them at the Beijing airport early in the morning. Eacher had little news from Paul and Rose's family and was surprised to learn that young Clare had already had a baby. Eacher had brought a handmade rocking horse for Windy's child. She was thankful for the gift and enjoyed sharing pictures of her baby, who should be able to use it in a year or two.

Windy traveled with them from the airport to their hotel. She suggested they attempt to sleep over the next 24 hours. She would meet them the next day for the presentation that she had arranged. They slept about twelve hours and made no effort to leave the hotel.

The first meeting was organized by Windy's boss. In that discussion, they met with Chinese executives interested in selling more wind turbines, solar panels, large-scale batteries, and electric vehicles to the United States. The Chinese dominated all four industries globally.

The speaker quickly honed in on the creditworthiness of the United States.

Eacher thought that the situation in the United States was improving and encouraged them to remain a strong trading partner.

The Chinese executive thanked him for his candor. He then pointed out that the United States had already borrowed a great deal that they hoped would someday be repaid. He paused while he let these remarks sink in.

Irene instinctively apologized for the delay but expressed hope that the United States would be able to keep up with its required payments.

This was the correct answer, and their executive looked pleased. The meeting ended shortly afterward, and they were returned to the hotel.

Windy scheduled them for a tour of The Great Wall that afternoon, and just after lunch, a guide picked them up and brought them to a remote section of the wall. The guide escorted them up the wall to an outpost where they could view miles of that wall. Irene was impressed with the scale of the effort to keep invaders out of China throughout their history; she wanted to walk farther, but Eacher was out of breath. They slowly returned downhill where their car was parked.

The following morning, Windy confirmed that the Chinese Industrial Marketing Association thought the United States could not afford to buy much more of its Net Zero related manufacturing output. In fact, the credit standing of the United States was so low, that the Chinese were essentially writing off some existing debt obligations that they never expected to be repaid.

This was actually a positive development from Windy's vantage point. Since that association saw little further market potential in the United States, they did not direct any communication restrictions on other discussions. Windy was even authorized to drop them off at the hotel and return to her office. The hotel could give them a shuttle back to the airport in time for the next flight back to the United States.

When Eacher learned this, he begged Windy to allow them to speak to a Chinese climate scientist. Windy made a call.

She drove them to a large concrete building. There were numerous pictures of wind turbines in motion and vast fields of solar panels on the waiting room's walls. Shortly, they were brought into a small conference room. It was an opulent room. A beautiful green marble conference table stood in the center, and a half dozen black leather upholstered office chairs arrayed around it. Energy infrastructure pictures were featured between several whiteboards. Small tombstone monuments celebrating successful deals sat on several shelves in a glassed display cabinet in the corner.

A young man appeared with a tray and placed a clear glass pot of green tea and some almond cookies on a side table near a window overlooking the entryway. Eacher and Irene appreciated the gesture and helped themselves.

Ten minutes later, Windy's contact entered the conference room. He was middle-aged, a little pudgy, and dressed in an expensive-looking suit. He projected the look of a well-fed, but important upper-level executive. He sat opposite them and motioned to them to take a seat. Windy explained the situation to him in Chinese, and he smiled.

Windy then described their background in English; this time, he nodded in approval. He hit a button. A screen slowly descended from the ceiling and a curtain deployed to block the light from the window.

"My name is Dong Wang." He said this with what sounded like a Boston accent. He had obviously spent some time in the northeastern United States.

"We are here at the request of the President of the United States," Irene responded.

Eacher chirped in. "Actually, we're here at Windy's invitation. We had the good fortune to meet her when she traveled to the United States."

Dong smiled. "I haven't been to the United States in almost twenty years. Not many other Chinese officials can say they've ever made the same journey."

"And there aren't many, like Windy, who can say they influenced the last Presidential election," Irene said.

Windy protested that she hadn't done anything special.

Eacher disagreed and described Windy's involvement in revealing one of the secret meetings at The Lost Woods.

The speaker smiled broadly. "Glad to hear that the stories were true!" He then quickly clicked out a message on his phone, put it in his jacket pocket, and gave them his attention.

"We wouldn't be here without her," Irene said.

"Fair enough; how can I help?"

"We're here to get your take on what's going on with the climate," Eacher said. "We have some aging satellites, but little beyond that. Most of our federal agencies have been gutted, and the funding has been dramatically reduced. Anything useful you can share would be of great assistance."

"So, you're not Net Zero enthusiasts?"

"No," Windy said. "Otherwise, our comrades would have never permitted us to speak to you."

"What specifically do you want my opinion on?"

Irene responded first. "Well, the most important question for our President is whether she ought to be concerned our about manmade carbon dioxide emissions in the United States."

"That's a smart question," Dong said. "Entire countries, including yours, have been entirely upended by their efforts to address that challenge."

"You're right," Eacher said. "It all boils down to whether decarbonization is something that we or any other country should worry about."

"What do you think the answer is?"

"No," Irene said, looking confidently at Eacher.

Eacher was a little hesitant to share his viewpoints. He didn't know enough about the background of the guy they were speaking with and didn't want to leave China without getting something worthwhile. He nodded his head.

"So, I'm speaking to two climate skeptics. What are the odds of that happening given the scientific consensus in the United States?"

"We've definitely been in the minority," Irene said.

"Even now?" Dong asked in an incredulous tone.

"I think the results speak for themselves. You Chinese sold us Net Zero gear the way the West once sold China morphine." Eacher said.

"That's an interesting metaphor." Dong paused and let these remarks sink in. "Nice analogy! You do understand that we weren't the ones that encouraged the developed world to pursue Net Zero? Even so, some of our government officials have tried to take credit for it."

"Let's not focus on those policies now," Irene said almost immediately. "We just wanted to hear your take on what's happening with the climate."

"I'll get to that," Dong said. "But if we're espousing deep insights, let me share one with you. Your country brainwashes your masses a little more than we do. However, in our case, we don't give them the power to act on their collective ignorance by voting us out of office. Allowing the central government vast powers occasionally bites us in the ass, as it did during the Cultural Revolution, but our elections don't regularly whipsaw our national direction."

"You're talking about global warming?" Eacher asked.

"Is there a better example of deliberate manipulation of the commoners?"

"So, your take is that manmade carbon dioxide emissions were not an issue?" Eacher said a little unsurely.

"Of course they were never a problem," Dong said emphatically. "It was always just one of many hypotheses that might have explained some aspect of the climate. It's the organization's history that gave the game away."

"How so?" Irene asked.

Dong stood up and walked to a whiteboard along the side wall. He picked up a black marker, drew three rectangles about the same size, and spaced them along a single line. The first one he labeled with "Physical Science Basis," the second he labeled with the word "Impacts, Adaptation, and Vulnerability," and the third he labeled with "Mitigation of Climate Change."

"Any idea what this is?" Dong asked in a professorial manner.

"Those are the three committees that the Intergovernmental Panel on Climate Change (IPCC) formed in 1988," Eacher said.

"Of course. China is a land of committees. We've got one for everything. Suppose we divide a problem into three sequential parts and simultaneously set them all in motion. In that case, we're pretty certain where we will end up."

"So you're saying that the United Nations chose this approach because they already knew the answer?"

"Better than that. The IPCC knew what the answers needed to be for each of the committees." Dong said. "Imagine if you're on the third committee and being asked to determine what solutions are available. What's your first question?"

"What's the problem?" Irene nodded her head.

"Exactly. In this case, what research did the third committee immediately start working on from the outset?"

"How to reduce manmade carbon dioxide emissions," Eacher said slowly. "Their job was to justify a mitigation approach".

"And what analysis did the second committee start working on at the outset?"

"What serious repercussions will the increase in greenhouse gases cause?" Irene said.

"Sort of, but that's close enough. Where does the second committee need to end their analysis?"

"They have to plug into where the third committee started," Irene said.

"And the endpoint for the first committee?"

"Where the second committee started," Eacher said.

"Even though their hypothesis is speculative and uncertain, how likely is it that any of the three committees follows a different path than the one they were tasked with?"

"I see," Eacher said. "Essentially the whole process is rigged."

"Rigged is a strong word. Perhaps a better word is 'preordained'? There was never any doubt what the IPCC would conclude with their assignments. It was a political process, not a scientific one. From day one, they have demanded that fossil fuel emissions be reduced."

"And China got a free pass because they were considered a developing country then."

"That was the only way we'd participate. Are you familiar with The Montreal Protocol?"

"Wasn't that the United Nations agreement to stop ozone depletion?" Irene said.

"Yeah, that's the one. It was signed in 1987 and entered into force in 1989. What's interesting about it is that the world implemented it almost immediately. Since ozone levels improved above Antarctica, it was considered a successful initiative."

"Yeah, that's what I've heard," Irene said sarcastically.

"Many international climate officials tried to pull off the same maneuver in eliminating fossil fuels. They met in Toronto, a different Canadian city, a year after the Montreal Protocol was signed and pushed hard for immediate action. They even issued a warning that manmade emissions were almost as dangerous as nuclear war."

"Can you imagine if they had actually been able to compel the world to cap fossil fuel use at that time?" Eacher said. "They would have taken credit for the 16-year temperature pause that began in 1999."

"Good point. Lucky for mankind, that wasn't a trivial feat to accomplish. While carbon dioxide levels rose as expected, global temperatures didn't. Clearly, something didn't add up with their CAGW theory."

"That does explain a lot of bad behavior from the IPCC over the years," Eacher said. "When their expectations didn't pan out, they were still committed to prove they had."

"Yep."

"But why go after fossil fuels?" Irene asked.

"First, they could measure increases in atmospheric CO_2 levels. These changes were very small, but they were deemed to have mostly resulted from fossil fuel emissions."

"And the second?" Eacher asked.

"Most of the world's fossil fuels are consumed by a minority of the world's population. Is that fair?"

"I wouldn't think so if I lived in a country that didn't have access to much energy," Irene said.

"It sounds like the perfect class action lawsuit," Eacher observed.

"Even better," Dong said. "Many that live in the developed world were ready to confess their guilt and pay penance."

"Sounds like a conspiracy theory," Irene said.

"Yeah, but it's not," Dong said. "I'm simply talking about why the world prematurely rallied around a suspect carbon dioxide hypothesis."

"What's your take on what's really driving the climate?" Eacher asked.

"There's been little research to investigate the other theories. We've taken the initiative in recent years, but there is much complexity involved. It's certainly easier to disprove a theory than to prove one."

"You must have an opinion," Irene said.

"Based on our analysis, I can assure you that carbon dioxide is not the world's thermostat. If you'll accept my word on this, what does it matter what specifically drives the climate?"

"I've long been a fan of the Winter Gatekeeper theory," Eacher said.

"Yeah, that's one of my favorites too. Perhaps someday in the distant future, we'll all sign off on that one. We'd at least have to get serious about preparing for the next hundred thousand-year glaciation cycle."

"Curious that those CAGW proponents predict that the next glaciation won't happen for another fifty thousand years," Irene stated just to hear his response. This was a concern that she and Eacher had often discussed.

"That is strange, isn't it? They try to claim that small amounts of carbon dioxide will cause terrible problems, yet ignore the largest potential climate problem of all. While we believe that the next glaciation won't initiate for at least another thousand years, that prospect is so terrifying that we're already working on ways to protect ourselves if it happens sooner." With those remarks, Dong stood up and motioned for them to stay seated. He shook their hands and headed out the door.

Windy left the room to check on the next speaker, and Eacher and Irene discussed what they had learned. Dong had made it clear that China found no value in decarbonization efforts. It didn't sound like this was a recent discovery. The Chinese must have known this truth for decades at the highest levels of their government. They invested wisely in their infrastructure and now sat atop the world's economic pyramid.

Most Chinese knew their country's ranking in the new global pecking order. Their congested streets and opulent lifestyles spoke volumes about their prosperity.

Windy returned to the room with the next speaker. This junior staff member focused on the need for more reliable temperature measurements determined by the rest of the world.

This speaker spoke about the Urban Heat Island Effect. China had gone to great trouble planting many shade trees within its cities. In addition, most Chinese had access to air conditioning at home, work, and public transportation. He asked whether the United States had taken similar measures.

Eacher grimaced and shook his head. "We used to, but few people can afford air conditioning these days. In addition, most of the nearby trees have been cut down for firewood. The people living in the cities during the summer, especially in the southern United States, suffer greatly from the heat."

Windy translated these remarks, and the speaker shook his head in disbelief.

Eacher smiled back weakly, and Irene tried to appear cheerful. Irene pointed out that the prior administration had moved many people into the country, allowing them to enjoy the cooler weather in more rural areas.

"Those efforts were done to protect them from overheated metropolitan areas?" Windy asked on behalf of the speaker.

"No, mostly to grow food," Eacher said.

The speaker looked shocked when Windy translated. "The United States seems to have a government that is not in their best interests."

"I'm afraid that's hard to argue with," Eacher said.

The speaker smiled in agreement when Windy explained this to him. "Anything else?" Windy asked, glancing between Eacher, Irene, and the speaker.

"No, that was useful, thanks," Irene said.

They were then picked up in a limousine and transported back to their hotel.

Windy and Kirk later fed them an expensive meal, compliments of the Chinese government. Neither Eacher nor Irene would ever forget the sumptuousness of that outing.

Windy then escorted them to the airport in time for a commercial flight back to the United States. She called in some favors and arranged for them to enjoy free upgrades to Business Class on the flight home, compliments of her government. They both thanked Windy profusely for this consideration and all her efforts on their behalf.

As the plane left the ground, they kissed and just held each other for the first few hours of the flight.

Kentucky Home
July 2038

L ittle Coleman cried loudly enough to wake Johnse's Mother, Linda, in the next room. Clare rushed to retrieve him from a small bassinet near the bed. She and Johnse enjoyed sleeping naked, and their door was locked. Johnse was still fast asleep on the other side of the bed, and Clare wanted him to stay that way.

Clare changed the baby's cloth diaper on a table by the window and then nursed him in bed. Satisfied for the moment, he fell asleep on her chest. She left him there and attempted to get back to sleep. Being a mother and wife was demanding, but compared to working in the fields most of the summer at home, it wasn't the most formidable challenge she'd ever faced.

This area was different from where her parents lived. There was a farmer's market where local produce was available, and there was no need to grow most of their food. Nevertheless, Linda maintained a sizable garden, and Clare occasionally helped out.

Johnse would be heading for the office in about three hours. He had rejoined the family business, but it was not the glorious edifice that Clare had imagined. It was little more than a few alcohol stills in a family-owned warehouse. Fueled by wood, it turned cracked corn, sugar, barley, and yeast into a very drinkable family recipe. The stills were large enough to create commercial volumes of moonshine sold or bartered to meet the family's needs.

Linda's other son, Billy, had been the lead brewer but had been tasting more of their samples. Johnse reassigned him to the delivery truck to distance him from their factory floor. Even so, a bottle or two magically disappeared each trip.

The reputation of their hooch had lost some of its cachet. The family recipe had stayed the same, but something needed to be fixed. The ingredients, how it was cooked, and possibly the cleanliness were different under Billy's watch.

Johnse's first step as a brewmaster was to work carefully and diligently from scratch. He followed every instruction to the letter, including distilling the well water before it was used. The result was exactly what it had always been. It took more effort but was still reliable.

In his first few months, he focused only on expanding the supply of the product that he knew was top-notch. This left him with much existing inventory that was not worthy of being sold as liquor. Instead of pouring it out, he distilled it to pure alcohol which turned it into ethanol. When finished, he poured it into five-gallon bottles for storage until needed.

He advertised it as fuel, and it was gone within a day. He didn't quite understand why it was so popular, but confirmed that it still sort of tasted like moonshine.

Government regulations dictated that an additive must be added to ethanol so that no one could drink it. Such additives made the alcohol toxic and transformed it from a clear liquid to a violet color. Lately, however, most of the regulators had been terminated and no one seemed to be too concerned about many rules, much less this one.

Johnse filled a small motorcycle with his ninety-nine percent alcohol mixture. He drove it about ten miles and then used a suction gadget that allowed him to suck out a small volume of the fuel. He tasted it again, and it had the same flavor as before. He poured the rest of his sample into his fuel tank and drove home.

Clare was washing some diapers in the sink while Coleman was napping. With a warm embrace, Johnse surprised her from behind, and she melted into his arms. He then sat at the table and waited for her to finish. She wrung out the last diaper and threw it in a pail. She turned to go outside to put the diapers on the clothesline when Johnse patted the seat beside him at the table.

He brought a small sample bottle and poured a swig into a shot glass. His wife looked at it strangely and smelled it. It reminded her of the delivery space where she gave birth; she wasn't sure what he wanted her to do with it.

He encouraged her to take a sip. She did so and started coughing immediately. "That's what your brew tastes like? It's potent!" She was still nursing and hadn't previously tried any of their alcohol.

"No, our moonshine tastes better than this; this is what our ethanol tastes like. I'm able to power a motorcycle with it."

"That's amazing. It's strong as hell, but the taste seemed okay – not that I know much about alcohol. I've never heard of anyone drinking ethanol before."

"It's fine without an additive." He then explained the story of how he'd further distilled his brother's failed concoctions to make this almost pure alcohol product. He described his brief motorcycle trip and showed her the device that he'd just used to extract the sample he'd given her from his fuel tank.

"That was taken from your gas tank? That's amazing. There must be a demand for this stuff."

"That's what I'm thinking," Johnse said. "Of course, that assumes they've gotten the gasoline entirely out of their fuel system and completely replaced it with our product. Perhaps we might even offer an inspection program to confirm this conversion."

He gave her another kiss and left her to her diaper pail. When he returned to the warehouse, he thought about various business plans. Who could he call to assist with all the particulars?

***

Johnse had spent most of the week brewing more ethanol. He had experimented with several methods, hoping to determine the most passable flavor. He settled on one that even his Mother enjoyed. He standardized that recipe and then discounted the remaining ethanol batches.

The following week, he started mass-producing the winning formula. Clare thought that he ought to call it "Aftertaste." Linda thought that name was okay, but given the history, it would invite too much notice. She suggested something more subtle. "Savor?"

"How about Savor Fuel?" Johnse offered.

"Too obvious. Just Savor." Clare said, smiling at Linda. "Most folks around here will think it's another way to spell saver." Coleman awoke from his nap with a scream for attention. Clare rushed to pick him up.

"Agreed." Johnse kissed Coleman, squeezed her shoulder, and returned to the warehouse. Neither of them liked to display much affection in front of his Mother. Given his age and her apparent youth, their affection for each other made many people uncomfortable.

When Clare finished nursing, Linda offered to watch her baby for the afternoon so she could join Johnse at the office to discuss marketing their new drinkable fuel.

Clare handed her child to Johnse's Mom and was out the door before she changed her mind.

***

Within a few weeks, the Hatfield moonshine business was back on top. Their traditional recipe was as popular as ever, and the dual-purpose ethanol had a small but growing local clientele.

It took them less than two weeks before one of their customers was charged with Driving While Intoxicated. The customer was a friend who swore by the product but learned the hard way that he had no business driving after he'd used it. A local reporter learned of this story, and the resulting news story drove a lot of business their way.

As their product sales grew, Johnse needed Linda and Clare's assistance in the warehouse and sales office with him. They hired a babysitter to allow them to spend more time at work.

Billy had a few minor accidents with the delivery truck, which had been converted to run off their ethanol. Fortunately, these were single-vehicle crashes that did not damage others. He was replaced as the driver and moved into the procurement side of the business, where he acquired the necessary ingredients to further expand their operations.

He would be gone for days, but his suppliers arrived on schedule. He was, perhaps, the biggest proponent of the Savor product in their family. Even so, for someone with his disposition to alcohol, it was a dangerous product for him to have access to.

Paul Visits a Collective
August 2038

Paul found himself on delivery duty. He was to deliver a wooden crate to an address that did not match his electronic map.

He found himself in an area about a hundred miles south of his farm. It was traditionally an agricultural zone in Arkansas for most of the last century. Large-scale farms in this area were once characterized by professional farmhands with numerous specialized machines. None of these tractors or harvesters were visible as he drove by. Instead, he noted what appeared to be gangs of workers spread out in the fields. There must've been 100 acres under cultivation, all apparently managed with hand tools. The operation reminded Paul of a chain gang that a local penitentiary might put to work.

Paul stopped his vehicle at the edge of the field and waved at the closest worker, who came over to talk to him. He directed Paul to the address he'd been looking for.

Paul then drove to the structure described but was still uncertain whether he'd located the right place. It was a tiny shanty, not much larger than a woodshed. There were no house numbers or street signs to confirm the delivery address.

Furthermore, it seemed doubtful that anyone lived in this building. There did not appear to be any electrical lines connecting this dwelling to the grid or other houses. Paul did note a wooden outhouse in the backyard, not far from the back door.

Paul parked just off the road and walked to the front door. He rapped lightly and listened closely for any movement inside.

A shriveled and bent old man used the door for support as he slowly opened it. Paul had to ask him several times whether this was the address he sought. When the old man finally understood the question, he nodded.

Paul returned to his vehicle and attempted to lift the wooden crate from the truck bed. It was surprisingly heavy. Paul returned to the front door and asked the old guy if it would be okay to pry open the box and only bring the contents to the door. After asking the question several times, the old guy just shook his head. Paul grabbed a pen from his pocket and wrote down his question on the delivery sheet. The old guy smiled and gave him the go-ahead.

Paul used a crowbar to remove the top of the box and learned it was full of ammunition cans. He removed them individually and then carried a few at a time inside. The old man got excited when he realized what Paul was delivering. This was Paul's last stop, and the old guy did not object to him hanging around.

The old man opened each ammunition box to inventory what he had just received. Each ammunition container contained numerous boxes of shells. The old man pulled the small boxes out of the large box and set them on his dining table. He opened one box and separated the shotgun shells, rifle shells, and various handgun bullets. He then pulled a box full of rifle magazines out from underneath his bed and started loading them.

Paul recognized that he was looking at a sizable ammunition investment. The old man seemed unlikely to have the money or arsenal to utilize these weapons. "These for your use?" Paul asked.

The old guy looked at him suspiciously but heard enough to respond without hesitation. "How's that your business?"

"You're right. It ain't. But it doesn't look like you can afford this pile of ammo."

"Look, young man. I'm too old to grow crops. But I still need to work, or I won't get any food."

"So you're kind of the neighborhood armorer?" Paul posited.

"Yeah, I guess you could say that. We got ourselves a collective here. A few lucky ones, like me, live in these villas while everybody else lives in that big house up yonder."

"You guys got property title?"

"No, it's a wood floor."

"I'm sorry, I said property title," Paul roared.

"Hell no, but the people that were here first didn't put up much of a fight. No one knows if they had land title either, and frankly, none of us care. The government wanted us here."

"You mind if I take a closer look around?" Paul asked several times before he got an answer.

"No problem for me, just be careful. We don't get many friendly strangers."

Paul returned to his truck and drove it to the circular driveway in front of the big house. He imagined it would look like one of those southern plantation buildings with expansive rooms. Surprised that it was simply a five-bedroom ranch-style house, he walked toward the front door while speculating what color this house used to be. Whatever paint had once covered the front face of the house had long been covered in grime or sandblasted by the wind. He heard a wind chime, sounding melodic tones from a minor breeze.

Children ran barefoot in and out of the open front door. The youngest wore no pants and squatted to pee next to a shrub in the driveway.

He tapped on the door. A middle-aged woman about Rose's age greeted him at the entrance. He introduced himself and explained that he had just delivered some boxes to one of the huts.

She was pleased with this information and introduced herself as Betsy. Apparently, their little community had recently run out of bullets, and everyone had pooled their remaining wealth to secure more. She also pointed out that her husband had been one of the casualties of a recent battle.

Paul offered his condolences and asked if he could tour the facility. She readily agreed and indicated that she would escort him herself. She led him through the entrance and gave him a rundown on the operation. The women mostly cooked, cleaned, and looked after the little ones. The men farmed, hunted, or undertook specialized labor. They all worked together to defend the facility when attacked, which seemed to happen with some regularity, but less often than in the past.

When she adjusted her gown straps to reveal more of her amble cleavage, her breasts almost emerged out of the top of her shirt.

Paul didn't think this was an accident. She really wanted him to stay.

"None of us have lived here for that long. We were all bussed or trucked here from various cities and dropped off without instructions. There were some families, like ours, but also clusters of unconnected people. I don't know who lived or worked here before, but that first year took its toll on all of us."

"You mean because of the fighting?" Paul asked, concerned.

"No, I mean because of the ignorance. None of us knew ditty about growing food. We didn't produce much that was edible that first year, and whoever had sent us here didn't seem particularly concerned. Do you know how to farm?" She checked her appearance in a mirror on the wall and then patted her hair down in places where it had been poking up.

"Yes, I own a small operation north of here," Paul said flatly, not wanting to share too much information about his circumstances.

This new information only served to encourage her further. She grabbed Paul's arm as the tour continued and brushed against it several times. She walked him through the house and kitchen and then noted all the various sleeping arrangements. There were a few beds, but mostly cots and hammocks. Every bedroom appeared equipped to sleep at least a dozen people. She pointed out the privacy of her bed in a small nook in one of the rooms.

"Congratulations on getting everyone organized. In my experience, that takes a lot of work." Paul said. "So the ammo I brought is for the hunters?"

"Some of it. The rest is for our defense. Too damn many marauders trying to steal our food supplies, and they've almost overrun us a few times. We started with much ammo, but almost nothing was left before you showed up. This little resupply of yours ought to keep us safe for years. Would you like to join us for dinner?"

There was the sound of a shot being fired out near the barn.

Paul was startled but said nothing. Betsy didn't act like it was anything unusual.

"Thanks for the offer, but I should be getting back." Paul suddenly felt uncomfortable but couldn't precisely pinpoint the source of his anxiety. He quickly excused himself and started heading back to his truck. He noticed connected trenches scattered around the main house. That was obviously part of their defense system. He also noted some sun-bleached white human skulls ominously mounted on posts at the edge of what must have been their defense line. Scary!

He glanced towards the barn. A burly man was about to use a machete on a slumped carcass that had been chained to a tree. There was a pool of blood that explained the gunshot that they'd just heard. The shoulder was cleaved in a single blow, and a muscular tattooed arm landed on a bloody sheet on the ground. The butcher picked up the appendage by the bicep and carried it toward a wood smoker already emitting a thick plume of smoke.

Paul immediately ran like hell in the direction of his truck. He didn't care if they saw him running; he knew it was time to leave. He imagined what it must have been like that first year without food. Clearly, they would have tried to steal the food from others, but is it possible that others became the food? He shuddered as he ran harder, his heart pounding in his chest.

He quickly unlocked the door when he reached his truck and scampered into his cab. In his side mirror, he noticed Betsy commanding several men to go after him. He noted them running in his direction.

Paul started the truck on the first try, squealed his tires, and accelerated away. He pulled his handgun out of his glove box and checked to confirm the safety was off. He waited for pursuers, but none showed up before he found his way back to the main highway.

He had just seen something he wasn't supposed to see, and they knew it. He didn't plan on staying to assure them that he wouldn't report their behavior to the authorities.

He involuntarily wondered if things would have come to this had the government not taken action to deliberately remove cattle and other farm animals from farms. He tried to laugh it off but had nightmares for weeks.

Won't Get Fueled Again
September 2038

E acher and Irene were sent to get an update on the nation's oil production. Jenny's Vice President, Tex Robertson, had suggested that they visit an active oil and gas field near Midland, Texas, to see for themselves how things were progressing.

They arrived mid-day when the temperature was sweltering, and they broke into sweat almost as soon as they left the plane. They were greeted by several rotund oil company executives. Eacher quickly surmised that they didn't live in the United States, where almost everyone he knew was thin. Those oil men loaded them into their full-sized sport utility vehicles. They transported them to an oil lease where they could observe some ongoing oil and gas drilling activity. About an hour later, they passed through a guarded entrance and parked near a 1,500-horsepower drilling rig next to several office trailers.

The staff assisted them in exiting the vehicle and handed them hard hats, goggles, and hearing protection. Larry Walters, the top company official now working in the United States, waddled to meet them and then escorted them on a rig tour. They ascended about a hundred feet up the stairs. Then, they entered into a small air-conditioned building known as a doghouse. They observed the rig operator using a computer toggle to manipulate various equipment to screw together the drill string one segment at a time as the drill bit advanced. Several roustabouts scrambled around the Kelly Deck before them, taking on supporting tasks as directed.

195

The rig was building 'the curve' part of the well, providing the drilling path between a two-mile vertical section and a two-mile horizontal lateral.

"There're a lot of pipe joints stacked on the side over there," Eacher noted.

"That's called casing," Larry confirmed.

"Is it new?"

"Yes."

"Do we make it in the U.S.?"

"No, we import it from China."

"Is it hard to get it here?"

"It was, but we're starting to work out the kinks."

"How so?"

"You're looking at about 20,000 feet of pipe for this one well that we had to move halfway around the world. That alone weighs about three hundred and fifty thousand pounds. We've also had to move our trucks into this country to handle those requirements."

"Sounds like a lot to worry about."

"You can't imagine all the trouble we run up against. Getting enough fuel to run our trucks and our rigs requires a lot of effort by itself. For every rig we have in operation, an unused one is nearby being cannibalized for spare parts."

"So, your major challenge is getting everything you need to drill these wells?" Irene asked.

"Hardly, the biggest problem is making business decisions on which risks we're willing to accept."

"You mean all those pesky regulations we've told you not to worry about?" Irene smiled weakly.

"Yeah, those things," Larry responded cynically and then continued. "That's where the business decisions get complicated. If the federal government requires us to conduct an environmental impact study for every well we drill, it would take us years to get a single permit. President Almond has encouraged the Texas Railroad Commission to green light our permits without it."

"That sounds like what we wanted to happen," Eacher said. "We can pardon those Commissioners if they get charged for violating the federal law."

"You're missing the point. You overlook how many people escaped the political craziness in California and moved to Texas. Texas is no longer a red state. That commission is now run by people who are no longer sympathetic to your party or your objectives; a number are essentially environmental activists. That commission doesn't want to issue us permits to drill wells."

"Damn, President Almond just assumed they would be supportive."

"Bad assumption. You can't protect us from the legal authority of a hostile state agency."

"I'm sorry," Irene said. "We were not aware that your situation was so difficult here. We'll talk to President Almond to see what she wants."

"Understand. If we can't get this sorted out, we'll finish drilling and completing the wells on this pad and then start winding down our operations."

"We owe you an answer!" Irene promised.

***

Eacher and Irene emailed Jenny on their way back to the airport to update her on the situation. She called them back about four hours later.

"We need these wells to come online. If we can't get more natural gas into production, our expansion is going to fall flat on its face."

"It's not looking good," Irene said. "Any chance you can speak to the governor?"

"I'll see what I can do. My bet is that those oil and gas wells would generate a lot of severance taxes for the State of Texas."

Later that afternoon, Eacher received a call from Larry. All of his company's outstanding well permits, pipeline permits, and facility permits had all been verbally approved; they'd be able to download the hard copy of the approved documents by the end of the week. Apparently, the oil regulators got the message.

***

Jenny was getting much feedback while on the campaign trail for the upcoming midterm elections. The United States had lost too much wealth over the past decade, and its citizens were now lower in the global pecking order for fuel. She was learning that gasoline and diesel were too expensive for most citizens.

Many people were getting excited about natural gas produced in the United States and transported around the country in pipelines. Domestically produced natural gas prices were about a fifth of the price of gasoline.

Jenny had an assortment of specialists working with pipeline companies to expedite the restoration of natural gas operations. It helped that the previous administrations kept the pilot light on some of the federal government's energy requirements. Some pipelines were old and had been terribly neglected. Those lines had to be thoroughly inspected, and any materials required to repair them had to be imported; this made them subject to long lead times.

As expected, there were a few explosions from natural gas pipeline leaks, and some people died. The media reached a lot of viewers by showcasing these accidents. Jenny personally appeared at some funerals but quietly notified her pipeline specialists to press on. She recognized that these activities were dangerous, but if the natural gas pipeline system couldn't be restored, that would be an even larger calamity.

The oil pipelines were also a concern, but since most of the oil would be exported, restoring those pipelines was a secondary priority for her and a top priority for the oil companies.

Convinced that the natural gas system could be restored, she asked Eacher to give her a better idea of how the vehicle conversion process worked.

At her request, Eacher set up a video conference with their contact, Dusty, who would walk her through the mechanics of converting a gasoline engine.

Dusty broadcasted the class from his junkyard garage. Jenny asked him many questions as she sat in front of a computer monitor in her office. By the time Dusty answered her last question, she understood how it worked. She asked him if there was anything she ought to know.

Dusty nervously admitted that he did not pay the required governmental conversion fees to the EPA. She thanked Dusty for his insights, promised him a pardon for the unpaid government fees, and ended the call.

Jenny turned sharply to Eacher. "Why can't the EPA just drop those conversion fees?"

"Great question. I guess my best answer is what Dusty once shared with me. The government has long been aware of the option to convert vehicles to natural gas. Those converted vehicles actually run cleaner than gasoline vehicles. Despite that advantage, the government had chosen to support electric vehicles and had deliberately discouraged natural gas conversions."

Jenny gave Eacher and Irene, one of those dumbfounded, looks that screamed that they had found another government attack on common sense.

She tasked them with figuring out which agency they needed to mug to get those vehicle conversion fees removed. Irene quickly figured it out, and Jenny effectively dismantled the portion of the agency charged with enforcing those provisions.

By the next week, Jenny publicly announced that the government vehicle conversion fees were gone. Activists rushed to sue them over this decision. Still, she would no longer support these provisions even when the environmentalists won in court, as they usually did.

Eacher called Dusty with the news, and he was not pleased by the change. He was concerned that too many others would now be competing with him.

On this point, he was partly right and partly wrong. He suddenly faced a lot more competition from many garages entering the engine conversion business. Even so, many potential customers learned of the opportunity, and he now had more business than before.

The biggest challenge for converters was locating the scuba tanks or other pressurized air tanks that could store the compressed natural gas. Once the vehicles were converted, the customers faced a challenge. The necessary gas compressors to pressurize these tanks to several thousand pounds per square inch were also in short supply. Home gas compressors were not cheap.

A call from Eacher and Irene to Windy seemed to make a difference. Within a few months, a flurry of Chinese air tanks and compressors showed up in the United States, addressing the significant constraints in making this fuel available. The remarkable thing about this government initiative was that no subsidies were necessary.

Demand for cheaper transportation fuel drove the market. Within six months, many gas stations had converted part of their facilities to compressed natural gas.

The Chinese also contributed to the solution. When they recognized the growth potential in compressed natural gas in the United States, they found creative ways to finance the compressors needed for the fuel station operators and also purchased several existing gas stations.

The irony was that natural gas vehicles were not widely available in China. Perhaps the primary reason is that much of their natural gas was imported as liquid natural gas (LNG); these prices were often linked to world oil prices. This arrangement made that fuel as expensive for them as gasoline or diesel.

Of course, the Chinese found a way to participate in this new growth industry in the United States. Within a year, they produced a range of natural gas vehicles for export. While these vehicles were more expensive than converting an older car, they were optimized to burn natural gas, which made them easier to maintain, more fuel efficient, and cleaner.

The Chinese government had also encouraged electric vehicles, but their approach differed with the path that the United States had taken.

First, their manufacturing sector led the world in producing electric vehicles and electrical vehicle batteries. Their EV vehicles were the lowest priced in the business and weren't subject to tariffs in their own country.

Secondly, they had built a lot of reliable coal-fueled power plants. Electricity was cheap and widely available to anyone who needed it. It advantaged battery-driven transportation and even helped reduce air pollution throughout much of China.

Protests
October 2038

A few rows of protesters occupied a small corner of the mall next to the Washington Monument. They carried placards condemning the nation's surge back to fossil fuels. The slogans were consistent with those seen in earlier Earth Days. "Keep it in the Ground. Save the Climate. 'Just say no' to more energy."

Many of the protesters were dressed like the hippies of old. They wore colorful clothes and vintage boots. Yet none were old enough to have participated or even likely to have heard much about the 1960's.

Encouraging an assembly of this size was a somewhat extravagant logistical exercise. In fact, when Jenny looked out of her window in the Oval Office and noted crowds of protesters assembled near the Washington Monument, she immediately suspected that this was a political operation.

She then tasked Eacher and Irene to determine what was really going on.

Eacher quickly found a costume store nearby that carried vintage clothing. He selected tie-dyed bell bottoms and a long-sleeved Dashiki shirt and wore an Afro wig the size of a medicine ball. Irene picked a brightly colored bell-sleeved shirt and a leather fringe vest. She also wore floral bell bottoms with peace signs etched all over them. She topped it off with a tie-dyed poncho, a long-haired black wig, and a velvet headband. It wasn't her preferred look, but they didn't have time for more shopping. They walked to The Mall in costume to infiltrate the visitors.

Eacher and Irene connected with a tiny group of college-aged students. "Hey," he said. "Some party?"

These events were so rare that this particular age group had probably never seen another protest before. Many students quickly descended upon them with questions.

They answered the students in rapid-fire mode. "Yes, there used to be Earth Days. No, fossil fuels are not against the law. Maybe the climate will be okay with more carbon dioxide emissions."

As they spoke, more protestors circled them to hear what they had to say. No one in this young crowd had ever challenged any climate dogma or ever heard of anyone willing to share what might pass as an honest opinion on this topic.

It was now Irene and Eacher's turn to ask questions: "Where are you from? Who brought you here? How long will you be staying?"

Several attendees recoiled from the inquiries and quickly moved away. Two older organizers smelled a rat and insisted on learning more about the background of these visitors.

The leaders weighed in with their credentials. One instructor had once participated in Greenpeace missions, and the other had once glued herself to the frame of a Rembrandt picture.

It was Eacher's impression that at least these two activists were not here as paid participants but as believers who wanted to make a difference.

Meanwhile, television cameras arrived on a van featuring the logo of a local television station. As soon as the cameras were on location, most of the participants stood up and started waving their placards with enthusiasm. The changing fall leaves and colorful outfits made for some attractive footage.

A spokesman for the group, wearing an open faux buckskin vest over his hairy chest, went to meet a reporter in business attire. The two of them stood before a cameraman with a small video camera not much bigger than a smartphone. The reporter gave them some softball questions that appeared to have been coordinated in advance.

"Why are so many people here?"

"We're here to bring attention to the disaster that the current administration has inflicted upon our country. Our country's previous efforts to implement environmentally sound solutions seem forgotten."

"Where are you from?"

"Each of us has come to challenge recent policy changes. As a nation, we have backtracked on our Net Zero obligations. With more natural gas and other energy sources being encouraged, our national carbon dioxide levels are increasing."

"Has President Almond explained her reasoning?"

"Not that any of us have heard. Our sustainable lifestyles are being polluted with hydrocarbons."

"Why have you chosen to come forward at this time?"

"Because there is a national undercurrent of resistance against this administration's shortsighted, selfish, and foolish policy choices. They don't enforce important environmental regulations. Clean, cheap, and renewable wind and solar energy electricity sources are being diluted by coal and natural gas generation. The efforts to grow food locally are being abandoned in favor of distant, machine-driven, genetically modified crops. At the rate we're going, it won't be long before the United States witnesses more record droughts, floods, and forest fires. The planet is in trouble, and we must never forget that our own sacrifice is the only way to reduce the damage."

"What's your background?"

"I teach environmental science in Europe, but most of the people you see here today are from the United States." He said with a German accent. With these remarks, the crowd surged forward for the camera's benefit. It cheered for the spokesperson who explained the situation to the public.

Eacher hung out at the event for another hour. He learned that many attendees had been given free transportation from their neighborhoods. They were also assured of a hotel room for the night - along with several meals and a modest amount of alcohol. He also watched cash envelopes being given out to each participant by name.

The expense of conducting this type of exercise was not modest. Supporters and allies of Ellen's political party were almost certainly footing the bill. In addition, Irene surmised that most of the funding was likely coming from outside the United States.

Eacher and Irene returned to the White House and updated Jenny on what they had witnessed. Jenny was already sitting in her office watching a news program about the widespread dissatisfaction that had led to today's protest. The interviews and featured protest groups were filmed with high-quality footage from the capital. The newscasts were transmitted to numerous television and cable networks around the world.

It had been well organized and orchestrated to cast doubts on President Almond's environmental leadership. It was less destructive than rioters burning down buildings and looting stores, but it was visually interesting and going to reach a lot of viewers.

Midterm Collapse
December 2038

Just after the national elections, the media quickly declared the results. While several electoral races were still too close to call, this did not change the result—even if Jenny's side won them all.

There had been small victories along the way, but the stark reality was that rebuilding wealth takes a long time. The availability of gasoline and diesel at more reasonable prices helped some businesses. Still, it was beyond the budget of most Americans. That was something she understood viscerally. She had aimed at an economic miracle that had yet to happen.

Yet the exit polls did not confirm her intuition. Her opponents had made this election about issues *they* had caused during previous administrations.

Her administration had been blamed for the hyperinflation that had occurred before she took office. Monthly bank deposits still showed up for older adults, but they no longer enjoyed any inflation protection, and their value was diminutive. None of that had happened on her watch, and she was doing her best to restore the dollar's value.

The other party faulted her administration for the electrical grid's instability, high electricity prices, and ongoing blackouts. Even so, grid reliability had recently improved with the restoration of a few coal and natural gas power plants.

One politician even blamed her party for eliminating the food kitchens that had provided a safety net in many major cities. She knew that claim had no merit.

Climate change had also been mentioned as an issue. Academics, the remnants of Hollywood, and environmental activists on talk shows regularly bemoaned her efforts to restore access to fossil fuels. None of them ever mentioned the benefits of doing so.

People had accepted much misery over the past decade, partly because they believed they were doing something useful for the planet. The return to reliable fuels made some people feel like their sacrifices had been unappreciated.

***

It didn't take long for the other party's control of the Senate and House to impact Jenny's ability to influence the government. Once the new congress was in place, she had zero chance of passing more laws.

She also expected to be impeached soon. The rationale for such a process was unimportant; the other side had the numbers to make it happen.

Ellen Gloating
January 2039

Mike and Dora were back in his virtual meeting room. They were waiting for Ellen to join them for a scheduled meeting. She was already fifteen minutes late.

"Who called this meeting?" Dora asked.

"Ellen did. She just wanted to impress us with her party's success in the midterms."

"Has she sent you a message telling you she's running late?"

"Not that I've seen."

"I wonder what's keeping her. Should I reschedule?"

"No, her party had a great turnout for the midterms. Let's give her a little more time." Mike said.

"Hi." Ellen said as she materialized in the room using the "Cheshire Cat" option. Only her wide grin was visible for about ten seconds before the rest of her body fully appeared.

"Entering with a smile?" Mike asked.

"Yeah, I think our recent election results speak for themselves!"

"Your team deserves it. How'd your party pull this off?"

"Ah, the midterms were exactly as I foretold. Four years is not a lot of time."

"It sure looks like you knew what you were talking about. Any major takeaways?"

"You know, the usual. Climate change, sustainability, and focusing people's attention on the few benefitting from the current economy. No one likes to feel like they've been left behind."

"Do you have a strategy for the next two years?"

"More of the same. There's no way that she can reverse my legacy."

"Are you sure about that? Some parts of the country are looking up."

"Where did you hear that? Most news outlets describe how horrible things are around the country. Would you be interested in contributing funds to assist our efforts? We don't want to wait too long to start working on the next election cycle."

"Seems a little early for that."

"Nah, the sooner the better. Let's start campaigning and force the President to spend time dealing with our viewpoints."

"Such as?"

"Almond isn't showing much leadership. Does she even have a four-year plan?"

"Please, don't underestimate your opponent. She's cleverly avoided many of the regulatory potholes designed to make a recovery more difficult."

"Yeah, but we've still got some determined bureaucrats that will do their best to keep her distracted. I think we're in good shape."

"So, what's next?"

"Well, I will take some time off before we kick off the next election cycle. I was on the campaign trail for eight months before this last election and wasn't even running for office!"

"No doubt. Any plans where you want to go?"

"Not really. Do you have any suggestions?"

"Well, I'd avoid Europe, Australia, and Japan. They all took a knee on the Net Zero front, and there's a lot of unrest."

"How about New Zealand?"

"I'd give them a pass, too. Most English-speaking countries haven't fared well in a long time. Great places to lower your energy footprint, but kind of crappy places to live. There are quite a few Caribbean Islands that are really hopping. Many wealthy people moved in that direction."

"Okay, can you text me some recommendations?"

"Will do."

"Thanks for your time; I'll check in again in about six months."

"Thanks. Stay in touch."

With that suggestion, Ellen blinked instantly out of the room like a switched-off lamp.

"So, what's your take?" Dora asked.

"Not sure," Mike said. "Things are happening that should have mattered more in the midterm elections. It's almost like people were just too busy to vote."

"Interesting. I've mostly stayed on this compound. Our bikers are mostly off the payroll; some of them bit the dust, and others left to do something else. Not sure we accomplished much with those efforts."

"That's the way it works sometimes. You do something you think will make a difference, but then it doesn't work out like you thought it would."

"Well, I hope she's right about the country's direction."

"Just in case she's not, can you send me some suggestions of things we should undertake?"

"Sure, can I send it to you in about a month? I need to do some more legwork."

"Yeah, no problem." With those words, Mike hovered toward the room's exit door and swung the door open with a wave. He levitated out of the room, and the door closed gently behind him. She had never seen him leave this virtual conference room so deliberately before. She'd guess he was preoccupied with something he hadn't mentioned.

She understood why he sounded so encouraged by the election results but couldn't figure out why he seemed anxious at the same time. *What was she missing that gave him so much concern?*

Stranger in a Strange City
February 2039

E acher wore the linen suit he had worn during his debate at The Lost Woods. After that debate had been edited unfairly and broadcast to a national audience, he had been tagged with an unusual moniker. He was now about to appear on a live talk show on national television.

Jenny had been punched in the stomach from her party's election loss and was still trying to catch her breath. She was supposed to appear on this show but sent Eacher in her place. His last television appearance was a sober reminder that anything foolish that he might say would likely get aired.

"Go," came the demand from the stage manager. Eacher walked onto the stage, greeted the host, Maryam Napper, and sat on her sofa. She was now back on her home turf. She wore an astonishingly attractive, low-cut, emerald-colored gown that embellished her figure. Her contrast with Eacher's cheap linen suit was striking.

"Good morning," Maryam directed at the live audience in front of her. "Today, we are going to have another discussion with the man that many of you know as That Moron." This remark induced some snickering from the assembled crowd.

Eacher expected this insult and did his best to chuckle when it showed up. Smiling, he tossed a brief wave at the audience for the camera's benefit, but inside, this nickname made his blood seethe.

"So, do you mind if I simply call you 'Moron'?" She asked.

"I'd rather you didn't. Just call me Eacher."

"Fair enough. Welcome to my show. As many of you may recall, Mister Eacher appeared on a national debate with the

213

highly regarded climate expert Doctor Charles Baker. The result was pretty predictable, but I'll give him courage for showing up for the punishment."

The audience laughed on cue and Maryam continued. "Mr. Eacher now works as a special advisor to President Jenny Almond. Any take on the midterm election?"

"Well, we didn't get as many votes in certain districts as we had hoped."

"Perhaps I can call you Captain Obvious?" Maryam was clearly being led by a small hearing device in her ear.

"No, Eacher is fine."

"Got it. How much of this most recent election loss do you feel is a result of your disturbing climate opinions?"

"Actually, this is a subject our administration has deliberately avoided during the past two years."

"And you believe that was a mistake?" Maryam asked in an incredulous tone.

"Maybe."

"How so."

"Certain climate science rationalized government policies that devastated our economy. Our focus was to reverse those policies and allow the economy to recover." Eacher squinted at her face as he said these words. The bright stage lights were difficult for him to get used to.

"So your administration has been furiously trying to restore our fossil fuel usage and convey people from the country back into the city." Maryam hardly noticed that he was studying her face; she was focused on what was being transmitted to her ear.

"Yes, those are two critical initiatives. A more sobering question is why previous administrations inflicted such harsh measures on our country in the first place! Fossil fuels provided more than seventy-five percent of our nation's primary energy when the government priced them harshly. At the same time, the government compelled many of our citizens to adopt subsistence agriculture lifestyles. Most of these people are now so poor that they can't afford to purchase many material comforts or utilize much energy. That was progress?"

"Those were important steps necessary to save the planet," Maryam stated confidently.

"You really believe that?"

"Doesn't everyone?" Maryam replied immediately, pulled the earpiece out of her ear, and dropped it in a pocket.

"Have you had much luck growing vegetables without much fertilizer?"

"I live in a high-rise in Manhattan. Even the plants in my condo are plastic." The audience laughed again.

"How do you obtain food?"

"My butler orders it online and keeps the refrigerator stocked for me. My cook prepares my meals."

"How do you get to work each day?"

"My driver picks me up in an electric vehicle and drops me off at the front door of our office building. Where is this going?"

"Well, I find it interesting that someone not overly concerned about the welfare of so many Americans is living pretty well in this new world."

She hadn't said, "Let them eat cake," but it was one of those moments where she was clearly out of step with most of her viewers. She restored her earpiece and sat there focused on the barrage of comments now being shared with her. Finally, she turned to Eacher and said. "What does my lifestyle have to do with climate change?"

"Ah, good point," Eacher said while nodding his head. "I had no business grilling you on your personal circumstances. You're a successful television personality and deserve to enjoy an affluent lifestyle. But is it any different than the one that most Americans used to be accustomed to? Why can't more people have access to food that they didn't have to grow themselves, comfortable lodging, and adequate transportation?"

"Yes, but you haven't answered my question about what this has to do with climate change." Maryam's insistence on this point made her sound assertive.

"The previous administration's measures to deal with our manmade global warming concerns were draconian. From my vantage point, they have nothing to do with what is happening with our climate."

"Then why would we take them?"

"Why don't you tell me what you think we've accomplished."

"We've lowered our carbon dioxide levels."

"Carbon dioxide is essentially plant food. Crop production is thriving at our current carbon dioxide levels. Besides, global carbon dioxide levels are rising at about the same rate that they've risen in the past ninety years."

"We've reduced our nation's energy consumption."

"True, but a fair amount of the energy we're no longer using is now being utilized by other countries."

"Sea levels no longer seem to be increasing as quickly."

"Sea levels have been rising for most of the past twenty thousand years and at a slower rate for the past 6,000 years. There hasn't been much change in the last few hundred years."

"But global temperatures are still rising."

"That's debatable. I've seen data that confirm that global temperatures have not been increasing in recent years."

"We've reduced extreme weather concerns."

"Most of these events occur at about the same rate as in the past."

"What about changes in ice levels near the north and south poles?"

"They haven't changed much. If increases in manmade carbon dioxide emissions were actually causing the polar ice to melt, we'd expect that the rate of ice loss would be constant and in only one direction. It's not."

"So, you've got an answer for everything? Do you even believe that there's been any global warming?"

"It depends on the time frame you choose. The world emerged from the Little Ice Age around 1850, and thankfully, there's been some minor warming since. We can't determine how much has come from natural causes and how much might have been caused by manmade carbon dioxide emissions. There's been similar warming in the past when increases in carbon dioxide concentrations could not have been blamed."

Her face was flushed red from her exasperation. She was clearly over her head on this topic and persisted in the discussion. "You see nothing wrong with the increase in carbon dioxide levels in our atmosphere?"

"No, I don't. We're in a brief interglacial period that may not last much longer. We should enjoy this warmer weather while we can."

Maryam switched her tact. "You'd prefer to make us dependent on hydrocarbons again?"

"No, not permanently, but at least until we transition to equally reliable energy sources. It's necessary to allow us to restore some of our country's economic vitality and technical capabilities."

Maryam reached up to her earpiece as if she were having difficulty hearing the ideas directed to her. She nodded slightly as if she'd just agreed on something and then faced Eacher.

"Well, great discussion, folks. Let's take a moment to hear from our sponsors." The television recording switched to commercials for the benefit of the audience.

Maryam and Eacher were asked to leave the stage and headed behind the curtains to their right. There, they were met by the wizard who was prompting Maryam's dialog.

"We're done here. I don't have the authority to let you go further." Winnie Martin, a beautiful and bright-looking woman, explained to both of them. She, too, seemed to have someone prompting thoughts to her hearing piece. "Maryam, we'll switch to the piano player we've kept on hold. He'll play his current 'Love that Plow' hit when we return from our commercial break. He'll then sit down with you and discuss his inspiration for writing it."

"Got it." Maryam looked relieved and returned to her seat on stage.

"Mr. Eacher. Thanks for coming. Hope to see you again in the future." With that, she dismissed him and continued to manage the ongoing show.

Eacher left the stage area, found Irene, and they left the building together. He hadn't said anything original or inconsistent with what Jenny had charged him to say. He allowed the moderator to bring up some climate science concerns and gently rebutted them without getting too technical. Most likely, none of this exchange would ever be televised anyway.

"It bothers me that we're getting such a hostile reception from the media," Eacher said.

"Nah, it's what they're compensated to do," Irene responded.

"You know, I think it's about time that we talk Jenny into letting us take on these vested climate change interests," Eacher said.

"It's an interesting idea. Do you think she'll go for it?"

"Not sure, but we just got pounded in the midterms. Jenny might be open to the idea."

***

Eacher and Irene sat in chairs facing Jenny, still behind her desk in the Oval Office. It was brisk outside and her thermostat was set low, so they draped their scarves and winter jackets over their laps.

"I'm sorry, but I have a meeting in fifteen minutes. Is that enough time to cover whatever you want to talk about? If not, we can reschedule." Jenny looked a bit tired. Her days and nights were relentless, and Eacher and Irene no longer got much of her time.

"I'm frustrated," he responded. "There are some ideas I'd like to get across to the public, but I need your approval before I dive in deeper."

"If you only got to share one idea, what would it be?" Jenny asked.

"Just one? That our country's Net Zero journey has been ludicrous."

She gave him her full attention. "Give me your elevator pitch."

"Fossil fuel electrical generation worked well in the past. Electricity was cheap and the system was reliable. Wind and solar power were never an adequate replacement and the eradication of hydrocarbon power generation gutted our electrical grid and crippled our country."

"Okay, not bad. Irene, what's your take?"

"I think the climate science that justified it is preposterous. The IPCC is a political organization, not a scientific one. It's biased and untrustworthy. Their supporters fudged the science, ignored dissenting research, and demonized critics."

"Is that it?" Jenny asked.

"I could go into greater depth, especially on general circulation climate models. There are around a hundred of them and almost all predict a dire future; if they didn't, governments would have stopped funding them a long time ago. In addition, the models fail with cloud parameters and other issues that make them useless for long-term predictions."

"Are there any other major issues you've omitted?" Jenny asked.

"Yes, there's a lot more material that either of us could have covered," Eacher said.

"Got it," Jenny said. "The answer is 'no'. You do not have my authorization to share your insights with the public."

"But…" Eacher said.

"No buts!" President Almond continued, "Most citizens in this country believe the other party's hogwash with religious fervor, yet know zilch about the actual energy dynamics or climate science. We've got less than two years before the next election. Now's the time to implement an economic miracle!"

"Maybe we can reconsider this decision next term?" Irene asked hopefully.

"We may not get a second term. I've got to get to my next meeting." Jenny stood up, stretched her back, and walked out the door.

Back to Business

February 2039

R ose missed Paul, but the money in their bank account now protected their lifestyle. With some of that money, she could lease a tractor and fuel. Operating it herself, she completed more daily work than they could have accomplished during the growing season by hand. She could also put more acreage into production than in past years.

Rose also missed Clare but received electronic images of her with Coleman several times a week. She and her daughter spoke frequently and Clare did her best to stay in touch.

Jose, Della, and Marie were starting to catch up with their classmates at school on academic subjects, and Rose worked with them at home to speed up the process. Their ability to fend for themselves in the big city made them street-wise and tough, giving them a survival advantage. One young man at school tried to bully Jose once and didn't make that mistake again.

When they first arrived, they were wary and unsettled. Rose would not have been surprised if she had woken up one morning to find them missing.

The longer they stayed, the less they projected the toughness they had maintained in the city. When they first arrived, Della and Jose were about the same size. Since then, Jose had a growth spurt and grew six inches taller. His upper torso had also thickened up, and he could manage tasks he could not have done before.

The local girls at school appreciated his increasingly athletic form. Some young women found some excuse to stop by and either assist Jose with his homework or allow him to help with theirs.

Della was a little younger than Clare, raising Rose's concerns about her interactions with boys. Nevertheless, Jose was protective and did not intend to give her the space to make a mistake she might regret later. The boys who might have dated her generally thought twice about doing so, given their respect for Jose's temper.

Marie had a nasty habit of pick-pocketing other students and her teachers on occasion. At first, the thefts were unexplained, but once she was caught, all the missing pieces fell into place. Rose tested her skills at home and found that Marie could lift her watch and wallet without causing much notice. She counseled her on the problems associated with this occupation, and Jose was even more direct. She eventually stopped getting caught, but Rose and Jose heard about it every time something went missing at school.

Jose set up a market stand on the road next to their house. A few winter vegetables were coming into season. In addition, Rose gave him canned and bottled vegetables from their food storage. He quickly discovered that they couldn't compete with the new price of foodstuffs at the local supermarket. Everything had gotten cheaper as more machines were used to grow crops and distribute food nationwide. They could still subsist off the food they grew, but the notion that they could earn much income from their harvests seemed increasingly unlikely.

***

Jenny recognized the creativity and enthusiasm that Eacher and Irene contributed to her administration. She also learned a great deal from the notes they brought back from China.

She was encouraged to confirm that there was no value to decarbonization. She immediately and confidently communicated this perspective throughout the entire Executive Branch and all of the government's agencies.

She also noted that electricity was the single most important enabler for her economic plan to be successful. The cities in the southern part of the country were so hot that if the locals couldn't access air conditioning or shade during the summer, very little would be accomplished. She chose not to add more shade trees in the major cities, only because she was certain that they'd get consumed as firewood by the end of the winter.

She also understood the reference to brainwashing. She was especially wary of the indoctrination that most young people had received; attempting to re-educate them on valid Climate Science was a stretch. Such a perspective would not be easily reconciled with the quasi-religious reverence that the chosen narrative enjoyed from its academic, religious, and media pedestals. She hoped that the dream of capitalism and freedom could still resonate with most of the country.

Conferenced
March 2039

Jenny attended a United Nations conference in Beijing. About ten years earlier, the United Nations had relocated from the United States when living in the United States became unpopular for foreign diplomats. She had been asked to present her plans for the United States to the entire assembly. She agreed.

"My fellow politicians, I come to you today as someone who is desperately hoping to restore some of the vitality and luster that many of you remember the United States for. We unilaterally gave up coal, crude oil, and natural gas, many of which were produced in our country, and also drove much of our population into the country."

"Go back home!" A heckler voiced from the back of the assembly. "Who asked you to return to fossil fuels?"

"Excuse me?" Jenny said firmly into the microphone. "Can't I finish my talk?"

"Why should we dignify your presence by allowing you to lecture us? The world is overheating, yet you want to return your country to the old ways."

"Excuse me, can security encourage this individual to let me finish my talk?"

"Madam President, that person is the Chancellor of Germany. She has the right to speak on behalf of the European Union."

"Then why was I invited to speak to this assembly?" Jenny asked, confused.

"Some people here care what you have to say, but most do not. We have all suffered from the consequences of manmade

227

emissions in one way or another. The policies that we have implemented have imposed huge costs on our economies, but we've accepted that. After making all those changes, you're setting a bad example for the more radical elements among our populations." The Chancellor responded.

Someone discharged a firearm outside the assembly. Security rushed on the stage to escort President Almond to safety. They took her as far as the first row and then just deposited her there. A number of the delegates clapped their hands when they observed the actions of the security staff.

Miffed, Jenny returned to the microphone and continued her remarks while the assembly settled back down. "The United Nations is imposing some type of socialist agenda on the rest of the world. In encouraging all of us to seek common levels of energy per capita, you make us poorer and limit mankind's ability to attain a more promising future."

This comment seemed to really piss off the Chancellor of Germany again. "Our country had a history of discrimination in World War I**I. We have disavowed our previous actions. When has the United States ever disavowed anything? You now seek to increase hydrocarbons while many other countries are still trying to lower global emissions? You didn't come here to apologize, you came here to lecture us on why you have the right to contest our political consensus."

"Can we discuss these issues in private?"

"We can discuss it in this forum. We should all hear your remarks if you've got something important to say."

"We don't need to abandon our citizens to inefficient agricultural practices to reduce our environmental impact."

"Why not? What happens if everyone follows your example? How long can the world withstand the volume of material accumulation that we've seen practiced in the United States for the last century? How is that sustainable?"

"Things are different in Germany?"

"Of course they are. We've undertaken several of the same actions that your previous administration implemented. We've moved people into hands-on farming activities, shut down most of our heavy industries, and greatly reduced carbon dioxide emissions within Germany. We get by on whatever energy our wind turbines and solar panels can generate, whenever they can."

"And that's a good thing? We might be democracies, but our people didn't choose to go in these directions; the governments did. How little you trust economics and capitalism." With these remarks, Jenny bowed her head to those around the assembly. She then left the stage and followed some of her Secret Service agents out of the building.

Jenny was not surprised to be greeted with such hostility. The policies implemented by her predecessor had been implemented throughout much of the developed world, with similar consequences. The countries previously considered developed had almost all suffered an erosion in their quality of life, life expectancies, and industrial capabilities.

The other forum members used their status as undeveloped or developing countries to refrain from implementing meaningful Net Zero policies. That did not mean they could implement the policies they preferred. Like it or not, many relied on funding from international organizations, which came with various restrictions. They would have benefited the most from following the same fossil fuel-driven energy development path the developed countries had once taken. Still, the United Nations used its forum to obstruct that possibility.

While China had assisted Jenny in the previous election, they had yet to take similar actions to encourage the other previously developed countries to follow a similar course. Jenny didn't believe they were against doing so but needed an invitation to become involved.

As Jenny sat in the back seat of her limousine on her way to her hotel, she received a call from her schedule coordinator. A Chinese diplomat was asking if they could meet before she returned to the United States. Jenny had not anticipated this invitation but dared not decline it. The meeting was set in a local Chinese restaurant later in the evening.

***

The designated restaurant sat on a small hill with a view of the city. When her entourage drove to the front of the facility, they parked at the front door, and several members of her security staff walked into the building with her. The Chinese had a significant presence of security staff of their own, and there were no other guests.

The room was festooned with paper lanterns and Terra Cotta warriors in various poses and uniforms. Paper walls and dark lacquered wood finishes lined all the doors and paneling along the walls. The dark wood table and chairs were hand-carved with intricate patterns.

The hosts sat Jenny at a small table. Her security team took positions around the room. The Chinese Premier emerged from a side room dressed in a black Western-style suit, white shirt, and thin blue tie. He sat down across from her and looked steadily in her direction. Several members of his security staff joined those already in the room.

"So nice you could join me!" He said in English in a warm and confirming tone.

"It's so nice you invited me," Jenny replied, not really sure what he would understand.

The conversation continued in pleasantries for some time. Jenny thanked him emphatically for their marketing assistance during her national election. He smiled and nodded his head but said nothing further on that point.

"I invited you to dinner this evening to get to know you a little better."

"I'm glad you made the effort."

"We live in a world that can't decide where it wants to go. We suffered through great hardship during our own Cultural Revolution. The Western versions we've witnessed around the world are recognizably self-inflicted."

"Yes, we came to that conclusion ourselves. Too bad we couldn't have learned from your mistakes."

"Had you done so, you would not have gotten the full richness of the lesson."

"True."

"Some part of the developed world is still committed to the same masochistic path. We were surprised to see you win your national election. We almost didn't support you because none of my staff thought you had a chance."

"None of my staff thought so either. Your assistance was incredible."

"And yet, here you are."

Not sure I'll ever fully understand why you were willing to bet on me, but our midterm elections did not go well. We're racing to take advantage of the small window of time left before the next one."

"Your last election didn't go well. Even so, my advisors indicate that your country has made some progress. How can we assist you to win a second term?"

"Nothing. We need to do this on our own."

"You don't need more resources from us?"

"No, we simply need to get the government out of the way. Allow our capitalism to work without all the punitive regulations and government assistance."

"You're confident that can work?"

"If we can restore our economic momentum."

"What about decarbonization?" He asked with a serious look on his face.

Jenny looked at him closely and said nothing. She continued to look, and finally, he just cracked up. "Okay, you got me!"

"Decarbonization!" Jenny laughed. "That's a good one! I knew you had a sense of humor!"

"True, but it really does help us sell a lot of stuff! Our big problem is actually air pollution. We prefer EVs, partly because we own the industry but partly because we're rich enough to afford better-quality air. The cheap combustion engine vehicles, especially with those crappy catalytic converters we were using before, did us no favors."

"So, you're not worried about climate change either?" Jenny asked just to hear it restated by this powerful man.

"Actually, I am. But, it's not what the rest of the world has latched on to. We're still in an Ice Age; the next glaciation could come at any time. Even sooner if some of these geniuses start to block incoming sunlight or take other actions to cool the planet. If that happens, things are going to be horrible for most."

"I don't want to even think about that."

"Neither do I, but it seems like a world where every country would need to fend for themselves. How can mankind make so many bad decisions when everyone's quality of life ought to be improving? The world is genty warming. Think how difficult it would be to face the difficulties of a rapidly cooling climate."

"How do you take something like that on?"

"We have a unified government. In our case, the government would defend our borders and decide how to proceed."

"I honestly don't know what we would do. Not many have given the possibility any thought."

"Let's hope that neither of us needs to ever make those decisions."

"Amen," Jenny replied.

"Please don't hesitate to let me know if we can ever be of assistance. I look forward to the day when our two great countries are capable of working together again."

The meeting continued for another hour. The food was truly extraordinary and not something that Jenny was accustomed to.

As she left the restaurant heading to the airport to return home on Air China, she mulled through her mind if there was anything that China could do to assist. She knew they could contribute resources, but also feared that it would be political suicide. No, this time she really needed to do without their assistance.

Legislative Assaults
September 2039

Tex Robertson had always been Jenny's best protection from impeachment. He was the guy who got to run the country if she was removed from office.

As an oil and gas attorney, he made his fortune putting together domestic oil and gas deals initially and then global deals later. Early in his career, he was involved in some of the earliest shale drilling plays. He secured extensive acreage in the most attractive plays before his competition recognized what they were working on. They concealed their lease acquisition efforts by utilizing third-party services that masked their involvement and kept their geophysical analysis a secret.

While the investors loved him, he had a reputation as a shyster. He was incredibly skilled at persuading landowners to lease their acreage on terms obscenely below the market value enjoyed a few years later. Many of these lessors were outraged when they learned how much money they had left on the negotiating table. Even so, he made himself, and a few ranchers who were late to the party in certain very productive areas, quite wealthy.

When the hammer was lowered in the oil and gas business in the United States, he moved to one of his Texas ranches, where he operated remotely. He continued to assemble early-stage international deals for oil projects outside the United States that attracted funding and top-level operators. He found ways to keep much of his wealth outside the United States. He supported several successful businesses around the world.

He dabbled in politics for a few years and spent some time in the House of Representatives. When Jenny was running for office, she approached him to be her candidate for Vice President. This was partly because he was willing to join her team and partly because he was willing to fund a portion of her campaigning expenses. He quickly accepted, though he did little campaigning himself in the general election.

So, shortly after the midterm elections, when the House of Representatives started their proceedings to impeach Jenny, she wasn't apprehensive about the final outcome of that process. This position surprised some, especially since Ellen's party had the required votes in hand that could end Jenny's time in office. Her only reprieve was that Tex was much less acceptable to Ellen's party than Jenny. Suffice it to say that she didn't lose much sleep over these ongoing theatrics.

Having served in Congress, Tex knew how shrewd and ruthless these particular individuals could be; it was essential to deal with them carefully. Tex spread the word that he was willing to testify against Jenny in the impeachment process if the opposition party needed him to take the stage. He seemed to favor a promotion, and some believed he would be willing to throw Jenny under the bus.

Ellen thought Jenny was beatable, as she had just proven in the midterms. She did not fear facing her in the next national election. Still, the opportunity to cover Jenny with mud was irresistible, and the impeachment process moved forward slowly and with feigned solemnity with her encouragement.

The charges against Jenny dealt with her recklessness. They impugned her for her willingness to distribute ammunition broadly and her failure to enforce numerous legal provisions that had been implemented by the prior administration. In addition, her blanket pardons offended many people and were being closely scrutinized.

Impeachment Committee Hearings were scheduled to last at least six months. Numerous citizens had lost loved ones to gun violence and dozens of citizens were invited to testify how they or their loved ones had been victimized.

There were a great many other people who had used their access to ammunition and weapons to stop bad guys and criminals and protect their families and property. However, no one from the ranks of the gun supporters was ever invited to share their perspectives in these forums.

Sad-faced environmental advocates bemoaned their numerous slights from ignored regulations. While it was technically illegal to sell new gasoline cars in the United States, slightly used ones were now being sold to those that could afford them. Most were coming from China, but some were coming from India.

In addition, bureaucrats from Jenny's administration who had been laid off were quite vocal and were frequently invited to be interviewed. They claimed Americans faced terrible dangers from natural gas stoves, water heaters, and dishwashers.

Natural gas pipelines that had languished for years were recently completed and were now in service. This upset those fixated on eliminating hydrocarbons.

The Securities and Exchange Commission under President Almond's leadership had not recently punished companies for failing to set out extensive financial projections detailing future harms from climate change. These criticisms especially resonated with certain environmental foundations and activist lawyers.

Overall, Jenny effectively ignored the ongoing circus that dwelt on the changes that had arisen since she had taken office. She focused on continuing to do what she thought was important. Without control of either house of Congress, she had not been allowed to pass a single law since the midterm elections. It looked unlikely that she'd be able to pass another one before the next national election in thirteen months.

When Tex was finally called to testify after all the lower-level bitching had been thoroughly aired, his testimony wasn't nearly as helpful as the Impeachment Committee had been led to expect. He voiced considerable support for Jenny's accomplishments. He made it clear that these specific actions she had implemented had been deliberate and central to the renaissance around the country. He compared it to the early days of the shale oil revolution. Investors needed to get moving to take advantage of the early window of opportunity to make a lot of money.

The committee members quickly shut off his further remarks. Through their efforts, he had gotten valuable television exposure that the media rarely gave him.

Anyway, surveys suggested that most of the American public was ignoring these proceedings. The impeachment committee voted to table this issue so it never made it to the House floor or the Senate for a vote.

After it had utterly petered out, Tex scheduled a news conference at the White House to meet with reporters to answer any questions related to the final determinations of the impeachment process.

None showed up, and he made no effort to gather any.

Food!
October 2039

The shipping industry was rediscovering how to distribute perishable food by utilizing large warehouses near major cities. Paul was tasked with delivering a fresh produce truck to several different supermarkets in Oklahoma. His mind rambled as he approached his destination.

He was traveling on an Interstate Highway near Oklahoma City in an eighteen-wheeler. Most other vehicles on the road were electric scooters, and he remained in the passing lane for much of the trip. The road was concrete, and many potholes had recently been filled with asphalt, so the ride was relatively pleasant and uneventful.

He no longer feared that his truck would be assaulted by motorcycle gangs. He was part of the operation that eliminated that threat and was proud, though still surprised, by the central role that he had played in that effort. The primary fear that he now encountered in the grocery stores was whether his vegetables would spoil before they were sold. Money was still tight, and people were not used to getting their food from retail vendors.

Jenny's leadership had allowed the commercial-scale farms to return to business. Access to fertilizer, pesticides, and fuel allowed their specialized equipment to operate efficiently.

Their transportation distribution costs were also significant, but their operational scale gave them a serious advantage.

Paul believed in sustainability. He was well aware that the food on this truck required more energy per pound than the fruits and vegetables that he could grow on his tiny parcel – perhaps a lot more. The labor component they substituted for

239

their lack of machinery made their homegrown crops expensive.

Horses would not have been of any agricultural benefit. They would require a great deal of hay and other feed that would offset any benefit one might get from their utilization.

As an economist, he recognized that what he was observing was Adam Smith's invisible hand at work. Prices and costs are the key determinants that satisfy consumers' limited budgets. If fuel is scarce, anything that relies on it will cost more; one would naturally assume that the market, if left alone, would balance the costs of all inputs and prices.

The last administration contended that the extra energy costs associated with modern agriculture were an externality they needed to account for. Had President Almond simply enforced the existing rules on the books, the commercial-scale farming operations would still be "tits up." If Jenny lost the next election, the other party was almost certain to re-impose their draconian solutions. Food would again become scarce, and the efforts to move the population into the countryside would continue.

Paul took the highway exit to Tulsa.

To be honest, Paul was on the fence regarding the United States' efforts to move more people into the country. Around the year 1800, the planet's population was roughly a billion. Soon, it would reach ten billion, which imposed profound demands on the world's availability of minerals and other resources. He didn't believe that everyone on Earth could enjoy the high living standards of the average Chinaman, though admittedly, those were still lower than most of the citizens of the United States used to enjoy. The United States was starting to try to close the gap, but so were many other economically challenged countries.

Wouldn't the world be better off if everyone lived like he and Rose? Life would be considerably more difficult, but wouldn't that be worth it in the long run?

And then a tricky question occurred to him. Would it make sense for his family to live frugally when others did not? Many developed countries competed for the Net Zero goods that China could deliver cheaply. China's ability to avoid implementing those Net Zero constraints at home while pocketing their profits abroad enabled many of their citizens to amass wealth. Those with wealth accumulated assets that required others to pay them rent.

Paul felt exploited by this change in national circumstances. The United States had once been near the front of the wealth line. When that was the case, its citizens could continue buying goods when prices were highest. That situation didn't really bother him before. Still, now that many others were ahead of them in line, he felt for those with fewer resources.

Paul eased his truck into the back entrance to Reasor's and parked it next to the loading dock. He called to let the store know that he was on location and waiting to unload. The back door opened almost immediately, and a staff member came out urgently, ready to move his precious cargo into the building.

***

Rose was in the middle of hauling some pumpkins from the garden to the barn. They were carefully balanced on a small trailer she pulled behind her scooter. Her phone rang with a unique ring that could only mean Clare. She answered it immediately. "Hi." She said.

"Mom, thanks for taking my call."

"Clare, I miss you. How's Coleman?"

"Growing big. Almost two years old and very mobile. Not easy to keep up with him."

"I remember those days. You were the same way. How's business."

"Mom, we're expanding a lot. Managing operations is getting more challenging. We could use some professional help."

"Are you asking for my assistance?" Rose asked in an uncertain tone.

"You know, that might work. Want to come and give it a shot?"

"You don't need Johnse's permission?"

"It was his idea. Now that our second child is coming, I will probably not help as much with the business."

"What, a second child! When did this happen?"

"Just found out!"

"Tell you what, let me see what I can figure out."

"Sounds great. Let me know what you decide."

Rose moved the rest of the pumpkins to the barn. There was still a little produce left in the field, but they had already harvested most of their crop for the season."

When Jose and Della returned from school, she asked them to join her at the dining table. The two of them threw their backpacks into their room and then returned to take a seat. Marie played outside with the chickens.

Rose looked from one to the other. They needed to figure out where this discussion would go. "I just heard from Clare that she's got another bun in the oven."

"That's wonderful, Mrs. Stewart," Jose said. "Is she coming home any time soon?"

"No, I'm not sure the travel would suit her."

"So, you'd like to visit her?"

"Yes, that's the idea."

"So, when will you be leaving?"

"Well, with Paul out of town, it's not easy to just drop everything and go."

"Yes, but Della and I could watch your place until you return."

"You wouldn't be afraid if I left you by yourselves?" Rose asked.

"No, we've been on our own for most of our lives. We now know how to handle almost everything and could manage it without you."

"You really think so?" Rose asked.

"Without a doubt," Della confirmed.

"What if I don't make it back?" Rose asked.

"Well, that's something we'd need to think about, but this is the closest thing to home we've ever had."

"What about your studies?"

"Well, Della and I could continue to go to school until early March, and then I could stay home and get the crops going. I'd need some financial assistance with the seeds and fertilizer."

"So you'd need to give up your education?"

"This would be my education," Jose replied.

They finished the discussion, and Rose caught Paul on the phone. She explained the situation, and he was happy for her. She belonged in the corporate world, and he'd join her when he could.

She agreed. She did her best to ensure that Jose and his sisters were prepared for the tasks ahead and promised to be available by phone if they had any questions. She and Paul would pay the property taxes and assist with the financing. She drew up an agreement for Jose to sign.

He signed it without reading it and assured her they would be fine.

Within the week, an alcohol delivery truck showed up and transported Rose to Kentucky.

Women!
December 2039

Eacher and Irene returned late from the office. Jasmine greeted them as soon as they walked in his front door. "Tough day?"

"No, just a busy one," Irene said.

"Where are you going?" Eacher asked as he noted her suitcase near the door.

"I've landed a position in Atlanta."

"What will you be doing?" Irene asked.

"Walmart needs me to greet people."

"No, seriously, what will you be doing?" Eacher asked.

"I've got an offer for an advertising job."

"You're hard of hearing," Eacher said.

"Not me. You're the deaf one." Jasmine said.

"Well, I suppose you're right. Thanks for helping us to make this place our home," Eacher said. "Any chance you can sign some divorce paperwork?"

"You bet. Time for both of us to move on."

"There was a time in our life when you were all I ever thought of," Eacher said.

"No wonder you didn't get tuition."

"You mean tenure."

"Yes, of course," Jasmine never liked to be corrected and bristled at his clarification. "I'm taking off. I'll send you a letter with my address after I get settled."

"Well, then, I guess this is it," Irene said.

"Yes, it is. Thank you for allowing me to stay. Not the situation I had anticipated, but the one I needed."

"I'm glad it worked out," Irene said. "You moved in during a difficult transition for our country."

"Got that right. Stop by if either of you are ever in Georgia." Grabbing her winter coat and luggage, she headed out the door.

***

Irene was out of town on a trip, and Eacher sat in a small booth at the back of a pub. He slowly nursed a Guinness stout in a small glass. Every drop of the black liquid took him back to his days as a college instructor, when he used these types of settings to socialize with students and other teachers.

The ambiance seemed tense today.

He noticed six or seven college student-aged young women catering to some elderly foreigners. The girls were beautiful and dressed in clothes that displayed some of their better features. The primarily Asian men were talking to each other in their own language. Another young woman sat alone and looked hopefully in his direction.

He looked back at her, and she stood up and came towards him.

"Did you want me to join you?" She asked when she arrived at his table.

"Will that cost me anything?" He asked out of curiosity.

"Maybe a drink unless you want more." She said.

"No, a drink is enough. Please have a seat. Are you from around here?"

She pointed to a glass of wine on the menu and the waitress headed off to the bar to get it. "No, I'm from South Carolina," she said.

"Really, I used to live in South Carolina," he said.

"Small world," she said in a bored tone.

He knew she was second-guessing why she'd even come to this table. "These foreign guys in the bar, are they from around here?"

"No. I was supposed to join the party, but one of their buddies stayed home."

"Do you know if they've been here long?"

"The best I can tell, they flew in a few days ago. Their money goes a long way here."

"Curious," Eacher said.

She sized him up. "Do you even do women anymore?"

"Do what with them?" He asked.

"Whatever you need," she said, apparently concerned about getting too specific.

Prostitution was illegal but not unusual. He sized her up and down. She was pretty and much younger than he was. She had the cold stare of someone who had spent many hours manipulating spreadsheets behind a computer. Perhaps she was an MBA or a Consultant? "Maybe some analysis?"

"Can't help you there. Thanks for the drink." She started to stand to leave the table.

"No, please. Sit with me for a while. I'll pay you two hundred dollars if you stay for another hour."

"That's not much money," she said.

"No, you're right. Please take off if you've got a better gig." Eacher returned his focus to the froth on his beer.

"Actually, I've got an hour, but that's all. I need to be at work early in the morning."

"So, this is not your job?"

"No, of course not. I'm an analyst."

"For the government?"

"No, for environmental lawyers."

"Really, what do they do?"

"They do their best to milk our legal system. Every time some government regulation looks like it might get reversed or eliminated, they pour in the legal talent to keep that from happening."

"Sounds frustrating."

"For who? I get paid well when we're working on a case."

"Are you on one now?" Eacher asked.

"You sure have a lot of questions," she said.

"You're right." He took a small, slow sip of his beer and gently closed his eyes. She wanted attention, and he would let her take the lead.

"Yes, I'm working on a regulatory challenge." She said after a short pause in the discussion. "The current government is trying to lower the fuel efficiency standards."

"I know the ones you're talking about. Those recent fuel efficiency standards were impossible to meet unless you only wanted to sell electric vehicles. The new rules were aimed at more reasonable goals."

"Who cares? It's just a paycheck."

"Do you ever travel anywhere?"

"Not me. All of my work is done at our law office. Those elderly gentlemen with my friends regularly travel back and forth to China."

"Well, thanks for the info. Here's the money I promised."

"We're done? I don't need to leave that fast," she said.

"Well, you're welcome to stay. Anything on your mind?"

"Are you with the government?" She asked.

"Busted. Why does it matter?"

"Well, there are times when I have something valuable to share. Is there any chance you might be willing to put me in touch with someone who could help me monetize that information?"

"Maybe. Can you give me an example?"

"I know a bit about efforts to remove the current President from office."

"Get in line," Eacher taunted her.

"No, seriously. I've aware of some very wealthy people using their money to inflict damage on this administration."

"Can you give me an example?"

"Those motorcycle gangs."

"Yeah, I remember those bastards. They almost killed me once."

"Someone in my office arranged for their compensation."

"Are you serious?"

"Are you interested?"

Open for Business
January 2040

Johnse was overwhelmed managing the administration. Based on Clare's input, he thought Rose's first assignment should be figuring out her job title.

Clare set up her Mother with her computer and company network access. Their computer consultant gave her administrative access to every directory and folder involving the company's business. Clare was feeling queasy, so she took Coleman home so they could both nap.

Rose immediately recognized that the business documents weren't well organized, especially before Johnse had rejoined the family business.

She couldn't locate any tax documents and surmised that this business was operating below the radar on a cash basis. By the end of the day, she had absorbed the primary financial and operational picture. It was a solid product but managed like an illegal moonshine business. Her instinct was that they had a lot of potential. Still, they needed to quickly legitimize their business to attract some capital.

Her last task of the day was sampling the product. Johnse took her to a back room. He poured some of their best liquor into a shot glass and the rest of the bottle into a motorcycle.

She lightly sipped the glass and recognized that it still had an agreeable taste. She also poured the rest of the shot glass into the motorcycle's fuel tank, and Johnse took her for a spin around the neighborhood. The bike had considerably more power than the electric scooter she usually used.

Later, she helped put Coleman to bed and slept well in the guest bedroom that night. When she got to the office the following day, a business plan was already forming in her mind. The almost pure alcohol they could make was somewhat less than the cost of gasoline. Many vehicles could run on it or use it to reduce engine knock.

Clare updated her on their thoughts on the fuel drink's name, and Rose thought it was a reasonable suggestion.

Fueled chiefly by exhilaration, she completed the business plan by the end of her third day on the job. She created a cover sheet suggesting she should be the Chief Operating Officer (COO). She emailed two copies of the plan - one to Johnse and the other to Clare.

After reading her analysis, Johnse wanted to make her the Chief Executive Officer. She was flattered by the offer, but thought he'd be a better frontman for the organization. Clare chose to be her assistant so Rose could teach her everything she needed about business.

The strategy was simple: Focus on a single version of the drinkable fuel product. There wasn't much variation in the concentration of the fuel mixture, so their focus needed to be on the taste and the logistics. This decision allowed the company to simplify marketing and develop various distribution methods.

One of the local gas stations was able to sanitize its existing fuel tank and pumps, and the first batch was used to fill up a below-ground storage tank. That station was sold out within twenty-four hours.

Surprisingly, the major operational concerns had to do with the impact on the neighborhood. Bums were loitering around that gas station and buying the quart-sized containers inside. Others were filling up gas cans. Some customers drove in on motorcycles, filled them up, and weren't seen again for another week. News of the offering went viral, and the central focus of the business was to keep up with the demand.

Rose made solid recommendations every step of the way, and Clare learned more from her mother than she had ever thought possible. Johnse, too, was blown away by her technical skills and found that he had to work pretty hard to keep up with her. So much for being in charge.

Their significant business challenges were dealing with vehicle shortages and relying too much on a shaky electrical grid. Rose added a natural gas generator that assured their availability of affordable electricity, and they were creative regarding the vehicles they could use for their operations. Two wagons with horses were leased to allow them to deal with the immediate supply issues; they were scheduled to be replaced with natural gas-fueled trucks when the logistics permitted.

Rose could feel that the economy was getting ready to take off. Their timing was perfect. She secured a small company share for herself and Paul using their limited savings and her gold coin.

She called home occasionally to check on Jose and his sisters. They had no complaints and never brought any issues to her attention.

She asked if they needed help paying for the electricity, and Jose simply indicated they were not using it very much. She was satisfied that everything was under control.

***

Jose had little interest in unplugging from the rest of society by becoming self-sustaining. He had been willing to manage the farm because it assured them of food and a place to stay. He quickly realized that the food situation had changed. They could buy anything they needed at the local grocery store if they had some income. They also had stored vegetables from the previous winter. Food was not a concern. He had other ideas.

He contacted some of his associates back in Houston. They were surprised to hear from him but even more surprised when he indicated that he now controlled a remote patch of acreage in Arkansas.

He offered to supply his friends in Houston with Salvia Divinorum, sometimes called Diviner's Mint or Seer's Mint. This psychoactive plant can induce mild hallucinations, feelings of dissociation, and euphoria. He vaguely remembered or imagined his mother sharing stories about her family using it for various shamanic practices where she had grown up near Oaxaca, Mexico.

It was well-suited for a particular southern Mexico climate but needed intervention to grow in Arkansas. While it's illegal in Arkansas, Texas, and many other states, there are a few states, like New Mexico and Arizona, where it's not.

The seeds he needed showed up along with a small pickup truck and some assault rifles and ammunition – compliments of some of his new investors.

He knew little about growing it this far north and spent much time on the Internet, getting up to speed.

A middle-aged couple was dropped off to assist and keep an eye on his operation. They erected a plastic greenhouse and used much of the house as a plant nursery.

Jose and his associates could grow much of the food they needed and purchase whatever they wanted from the grocery store. Marie and Della still attended school and only had to do a few chores.

From the vantage point of a casual visitor, Jose appeared to be simply in the potted plant business. He felt good being an entrepreneur, especially in what he believed might have once been the family business.

Holding Court
March 2040

Jenny was on the campaign trail most days. She traveled primarily in a limousine convoy throughout the country, especially through the major cities. Fortunately, no one in her party challenged her, so she had already declared herself the winner of her party's Primary.

Ellen Winthrop and a few no-name candidates from the other party were opposing her. Effectively, she and Ellen were already campaigning against each other. It was a rematch of the current President against the prior President.

Ellen started wearing green pantsuits and talking continuously about clean energy. In her campaign ads, she featured prominent climate scientists. She quoted high-level figures from the IPCC who espoused that the world was at risk of overheating; they also projected that sea levels were likely to rise several feet over the next four years if she didn't get elected.

Once again, Ellen focused on the importance of her national de-growth strategy. Her party's stalwarts were the custodians of the planet. She wanted the United States to work with other countries to minimize mankind's influence on the natural world. This entailed reinstating her small farm strategy, reintroducing a carbon tax, and the promise that the United States would end the use of fossil fuels once and for all. After she took office, she assured voters that even the federal government would be forced to shut down their fossil fuel usage.

It was a simple strategy. Implement even more aggressive Net Zero policies. She didn't know if the federal government could function without all the back-door fossil fuel access, but they'd all find out if she got elected.

***

Jenny viewed Ellen's updated vision as an alarming development. Had it not been for the clandestine fossil fuels allowed under Ellen's administration, the country would have already disintegrated. How could the country operate without the large-scale farms, the relocation business, and all levels of government getting "preferential treatment"? The stakes in this election were even higher than she had previously imagined.

Furthermore, Jenny's strategy of allowing the private sector to operate with minimal government interference had been succeeding. The cities were showing some signs of life. Employment was picking up in some areas, and many had elected to leave the subsistence farming business and return to more productive occupations.

They'd lose the next Presidential election if her party couldn't pull more people out of poverty. Circumstances were now better for many, not just a few. If she could win this election and give the country another four years of dominance by the private sector, she was confident that the United States would escape their economic doldrums.

Ellen's plan was remarkable because of the honest way that she sold it. The media followed her lead and filmed her impromptu speeches around the clock. She appealed to unhappy citizens throughout the country. If they weren't better off, why should anyone be?

What was true was that the oil and gas companies were back in business in the United States, at least until the next election. As anticipated, the oil was primarily shipped abroad, and the natural gas was mainly consumed domestically. Various taxes filtered into the federal and a few state treasuries.

Some crude oil was refined in the United States so that jet fuel was available for airports. Filling stations still served minor volumes of gasoline and diesel. Still, their primary revenue increasingly came from selling natural gas.

Most importantly, spare parts were becoming more available. This development allowed many broken vehicles and various machines to be repaired. This was critical since so many cars had been sold abroad, and there weren't many used gasoline vehicles left in the country that could be converted. This initiative would take time but showed considerable promise.

Funds were starting to trickle in from outside the country. Some aimed to take advantage of the United States' economic growth prospects. Others were aimed at activists committed to stopping or reversing recent developments.

Most of the wealthy who had remained in the country were no longer wealthy. In this new economy, some might eventually be able to regain their lost wealth, but they weren't in a strong position to make many donations at the current time.

Jenny insisted that there could only be one path that would work. Let the economy take off in whatever direction it wanted to go and compel the government to get out of the way.

Liftoff
April 2040

E llen screamed at one of her economic advisors. "Are you serious? There is no way the national GDP has grown by ten percent over the last year! Who is in charge of these numbers?"

"President Winthrop, I can't explain it. I spent most of the last few days checking these numbers myself. They seem to be correct."

"More than twenty percent of our rural population has returned to the cities. Why aren't we seeing higher unemployment numbers?"

"Many of those in the city seem to be working in some capacity. There are lots of new companies starting businesses that need many workers."

"How is that possible?" Ellen asked in amazement. "Federal requirements don't allow companies to be easily organized."

"President Almond has ignored those constraints."

"How is that even possible? Her job as the Chief Executive is to enforce the laws and the rules."

"Not in this case. Wild West has pardoned most people that violated any rules that she considered unreasonable. She has terminated so much of the federal staff that there literally aren't enough people to enforce anything."

"This is absurd. We are a nation of law-abiding citizens, and ignoring the rules is not an option. Maybe we should run on that platform?"

"Maim, I don't recommend that we bring attention to it. There is a spirit that anything is possible underlining many of these changes. Non-enforcement has been remarkably popular. You and I know that most things they're not enforcing are unnecessary. The process to eliminate them is tedious, time-consuming, and dominated by highly paid lawyers."

"So you're suggesting that all these organizations have simply walked around the roadblocks we put in place?"

"Yes, that about sums it up."

"But, we won the midterm elections. How did we lose our momentum to restore the country to where it was at the end of my term?"

"Madam President, we were well prepared to defend the impenetrable regulatory thickets that had been put in place. It's simply that she kept her distance."

"Where the hell did they get all the vehicles?"

"Some were pieced together in the junkyards. A number of used cars were transported here by ship. More affordable electricity also attracted some inexpensive Chinese electric automobiles in various cities."

"The electrical grid, how did they put so many power plants back in operation?"

"The elimination of carbon taxes and more favorable rules for natural gas electricity generation were the central enablers. Since the major natural gas pipelines were surprisingly intact, filling those pipelines didn't take long, and several dozen mothballed facilities were returned to operation."

"So, what you're telling me is that the electrical grid is much more adequate for what's happening?"

"Yes. Part of the grid has returned to the days when fossil-fueled power plants were money makers."

"But what about all the people we unplugged from our economy?"

"Food is readily available in the supermarkets. Fewer people are afraid of starving and consequently are willing to take chances on employment opportunities."

"Now, I've heard of everything. Do you know how much work it will take to get this country back on track after I'm elected?"

"Quite a bit, it would seem."

"So, what issues will put me in office?"

"I'm sorry, but I'm not aware of any."

"Are you sure about that?"

"Most of the guns and ammo deputized ordinary citizens to protect their own assets, which I've been discretely assured has considerably reduced crime. The food kitchen program is no longer needed because most transients have returned to work. Most of them can now afford to buy their own food. Many are apparently leasing apartments." He stopped to take a breath.

"Is that how you see things?"

"Perhaps our best bet is to point at our alignment with the global leadership in the United Nations and the other formerly developed countries still trying to chase their Net Zero aspirations?"

"Okay, let's focus on that tact. There are plenty of people still willing to sacrifice to save the climate. Furthermore, I'm a celebrity, and people will vote for me simply because they know who I am."

"Great. Let's showcase you looking presidential and shaking hands with other world leaders. I'm sure we can resurrect some footage from the archives. What about personal attacks on Jenny?"

"What dirt do you have?"

"There are a lot of disgruntled federal employees that we can interview. In addition, the motorcycle gangs that were attacked can be depicted as victims. We can accuse her of an affair with one of the members of her staff."

"Really, which one?"

"She spends a lot of time with one simply known as Eacher. If we can piece enough footage of them together, we can spread a lot of innuendo."

"All right. Let's make that happen!" Ellen cried. Time to put together a winning campaign."

***

Eacher was sitting at a shoeshine stand not far from his apartment. He was getting his shoes shined on a lark; it was the first shoeshine boy he'd seen in years. The young man with the shoeshine equipment was doing a competent job on his shoes.

"Hey, mister. You know anything about buying stock?"

"There's not much to it. You pick a brokerage, and they will buy it for you."

"You own any stock?"

"Actually, no. Everything I had in the market went bust."

"Was that recently?"

"No, it was about fifteen years ago."

"Hmm, well, let me give you a stock tip. Drinkable Fuel. It's a new listing on the NASDAQ. I've tried their product, and it's quite a kicker."

"Thanks. I'll keep that in mind."

As Eacher returned to his apartment, he noted "For Sale" signs on several houses. Back in his room, he pulled out his computer and noted the upward direction of the stock market and local real estate prices. The numbers were difficult to interpret, given the persistent inflation. Still, one thing was clear, asset values were surging.

He knew about a recent influx of foreign capital into the US. The availability and affordability of electricity, transportation, and an educated workforce enabled many companies to compete for capital.

More importantly, all those service jobs, like hairdressers, food servers, or maids, started to pay more when the demand for these services increased from better-paid workers in the economy. A rising tide lifts all boats.

The dollar was now holding its own against the Chinese Yuan.

The US was no longer a doormat. Even so, it would take decades of similar growth to move back into the ranks of the world's second-tier countries. China was the dominant power and it wasn't slowing down. The US would be well advised to maintain them as an ally

Calling in the Calvary
May 2040

Mike and Dora met Ellen in their virtual meeting room. This time, Ellen brought several staff members into the meeting with her.

The view out the window was taken from high above the ground, perhaps from a balloon. Mike had selected this view, which made the room seem like they were flying somewhere. Dora couldn't stand to look out the window.

"What funds do you need from us to allow you to win the upcoming election?" Mike asked.

"We had this discussion before. I need you to spend enough money to ensure the media will be on our side." Ellen replied.

"And how would you characterize your advantage at the moment?" Mike asked.

"The country is still in a primitive state. Electricity and transportation have made some progress, but not enough. The current economic situation is chaotic. People want to return to less volatile times. The government fails to support regulatory authority. We are the laughingstock of the rest of the world. Time for us to rejoin the world community." Ellen said.

Mike clapped his hands several times in mock applause. "Bravo, you haven't lost your touch."

"Are you being snarky?"

"Of course. Isn't it called for?" He turned to face one of the advisors that Ellen had brought. "Mr. Whittington, you did a lot of financial analysis during the previous administration. What are your thoughts on the points that former President Winthrop just made."

"This messaging is consistent with what the media is regularly communicating to the public."

"I see," Mike said, facing the other advisor. "And you, is it Mr. Song?"

"Yes," he replied

"What do *you* think?"

"This messaging has enabled us to attract funding from our major donors."

"Yes, but do *you* agree?"

"They are powerful talking points."

"Well, perhaps they are. Even so, if the economy is in such rough shape, why would either of you bet on it?"

Both gentlemen looked at the former President and lowered their heads.

"What?" Ellen exclaimed. "Are you serious? What did you buy?"

"I acquired some industrial stocks." Mr. Song said.

"And you?" Mike stared hard at Mr. Whittington.

"I haven't bought any stock."

"Okay, that's consistent with my intelligence," Mike said.

"I've been purchasing corporate debt denominated in our currency." Mr Whittington said.

"What?" Ellen said. "You're betting that the dollar will appreciate?"

"I'm sorry, Madam President. I have."

"Why would you?"

"I'd rather not say." He avoided making eye contact with her.

"You'd better damn well say, or you're off my staff, Mr. Whittington."

"The debt I've been acquiring has been heavily discounted. If the companies that floated it in the first place return to financial solvency, then I'm going to make a killing."

"And you did this while you were working for me?"

"I'm sorry, I should have mentioned what I was doing."

"No, please, explain why you believe this type of gamble is good in this economy."

"I've already tripled my original investment over the past few months. The economy is flashing a lot of encouraging signs."

"Are there any other insights you want to share?" Ellen said with some incredulity.

"I'm guessing that scads of foreign investors will move into our stock market soon. I'd like to acquire a large position before those other players weigh in." Mr. Whittington continued.

"What do you think my chances are of getting elected?" Ellen asked, still in shock.

"I'm sorry, Madam President, but I wouldn't vote for you. There is no value in occupying so much of our country in busy work. Your vision of this country's future is not mine. I resign." He instantly vanished from their virtual conference room.

Mr. Song looked over at the empty seat and then at the others in the room. "Sorry, me too. Good luck with your election." With those remarks, he also disappeared.

Ellen looked very disturbed. Her ordinarily calm and self-assured demeanor seemed crestfallen.

Mike just sat there saying nothing. He closed his eyes, which only happens deliberately in a virtual meeting room. Most of the avatars don't blink.

Dora looked up. "How would you like to proceed?"

It wasn't clear whether she was asking this question of Mike or Ellen. Perhaps it didn't matter.

Ellen fielded it. "Thank you for pointing out the flaws in some of my key staff members. Their lack of loyalty might have cost me the election had you not pointed out their treachery. With your funding, I assure you the election is in the bag."

Mike looked up, turned, and faced her. "Ellen, those advisors didn't abandon you. They simply spoke honestly about what they've seen happening across the nation. I don't recommend that you rehire them or anyone else. This country is returning to economic viability."

"I agree that what is happening is popular. However, it's still unacceptable. A materially driven world is not sustainable."

"I agree with your assessment. It's just that the direction you still want to go does not seem possible. At least not at this moment."

"Have you considered that we could assassinate President Almond?"

Dora requested that she be allowed to leave the meeting.

Mike waved her off. She blinked out and was gone.

Mike sat facing Helen and pressed a button. The room transformed from a conference room into a small room, with the two of them facing each other across a small round table with a lit chess board. They were surrounded by dark walls, a blackened ceiling, and an ebony wood floor. Mike just sat mutely in his chair, staring at her.

Ellen finally spoke. "Look, what has happened could not have been predicted. Jenny avoided the weight of the bureaucracy by staying clear of it. I don't see how I can win at this juncture without considerable foul play. In time, her current strategy will fall short and it will be up to others to set things right."

"Sounds like *you* don't believe you can win?" Mike let this sink in and then continued. "Honestly, I don't believe you can either. I wish you luck. Just for the record, don't even consider assassinating your opponent; were you to succeed it might turn her into a martyr." Mike hit a second button, and the virtual room closed altogether.

Ellen found herself sitting alone in her home office. She looked down at the paper pad before her and checked Mike's name off the list.

A Canned Broadcast
August 2040

Ellen walked around the stage in a magnificent designer dress, an impressive pearl necklace, and diamonds glittering from her ears and fingers. Her appearance and expressions exuded power and success. She seemed to be waiting for someone to confirm that she was now the nation's top elected official again. She projected that she was waiting for her coronation, not mired in a fight for political survival.

With this audience, a handpicked assembly of strong supporters, the auditorium was rocking from the noise of their enthusiasm. They cheered when she walked on stage, applauded when she acknowledged their support, and continued to roar even after she took her seat.

Maryam Napper, the moderator, sat in a chair on stage facing her, with numerous cameras capturing multiple angles. It was a casual event, to be sure, but one in which Ellen had invested some serious campaign funds, trying to achieve just the right tone for this discussion.

Ellen stood up again to acknowledge the excitement. The audience grew even louder. "Thank you." She said. The noise continued another minute longer. Ellen motioned once for the sound to abate, and the room quieted.

"How is the campaign going?" Maryam asked.

"You see the energy that people have for my campaign." With that, the room erupted again for another thirty-second acclaim.

"Impressive. Is it always like this?"

"Pretty amazing, huh?"

"I've never seen anything similar. Why do you think there's such a groundswell for you?"

"I think it has much to do with the urgency to restore our country to a sound footing. Since we currently have a president who fails to enforce government regulations, why would you expect it to be otherwise? There's a reason she's nicknamed Wild West Jenny. Think of all the shootouts around the country where people are taking the law into their own hands. It's crazy!"

"You're right. There's been so much violence. Remember the story about the motorcycle club heading to a rally that was shot up by the police?"

"That is one of my favorite illustrations of the lawlessness we've seen over the past four years," Ellen said.

"Are you worried about the climate?"

"Terrified! Now that the United States is burning more coal, oil, and natural gas again, there is little doubt in my mind that we will cause the world to overheat. I mean, just follow the science. More greenhouse gases mean more warming. It's that simple."

"We haven't heard much discussion on these issues in the last few years."

"Well, we should have! When it comes to climate science, there is still a scientific consensus. As we all know, more greenhouse gas emissions will melt the ice at the poles, resulting in higher sea levels worldwide. Further, as the tundra and methane hydrates melt, even greater levels of greenhouse gases will be driven into the atmosphere. Last year was the hottest year ever!"

"So, clearly, our nation needs to be taking actions to reduce our use of hydrocarbons, not expand them," Maryam said.

"Absolutely. When we moved a large portion of our population into the country, we weren't just concerned about climate change. We were concerned with excess materialism. Our planet has too many people, and we should not be wasting resources that will not then be available to support our grandchildren and their grandchildren. We all must practice a healthy respect for the environment and steer clear of materialism."

"Many people are moving back from the country into the cities. Is this a healthy trend for our nation?"

"When I was President, I can't tell you how many people came up to me to tell me how happy they were to do their part to reduce the burden on the planet. It is just the way Americans are. We are willing to do without and go to great lengths to make the world better."

"Would you like to comment on your major initiatives if you're elected President again?"

"I love sharing my insights with our national audience. I intend to give the American people the clean energy they deserve. I want our elderly to have assistance with their medical needs and pensions so that they can live long and healthy lives without needing to work in their later years. We need to put the American people first."

"Why do you think you lost the last Presidential election?"

This wasn't a question that Ellen had prepared for. She didn't remember it being on her list. She thought quickly about how to respond. "If I remember rightly, the Chinese stepped in and provided some election funding and media assistance to Wild West's campaign."

"President Almond received political funding from foreign nations?"

"Yes, the Chinese are good at caring for their interests. In case you haven't noticed, Wild West Jenny is also good at caring for their interests."

The program continued in this spirit for the next fifteen minutes. Ellen never really explained which policies would benefit the demographic groups that she wanted to help. However, since she provided all the questions to the moderator in advance, she seamlessly slanted her responses in a favorable direction.

At the end of the broadcast, Maryam stood up and raised Ellen's arm as if she had just won a prize fight. Ellen looked triumphant as the show ended.

Ellen followed this format for the rest of the election cycle. She refused to debate or answer questions from any members of the media who were not being compensated by her campaign.

Shot Over
October 2040

Two figures were dressed in dark black Ninja dress with dark veils covering the lower portion of their faces. With long samurai blades slung behind their back, they were barely visible in the late evening.

One of the Secret Service agents had just taken a slow stroll outside the second-floor motel room where former President and current Presidential Candidate Ellen Winthrop was sleeping.

Two shadows slid down the roof and under the parapet directly in front of Ellen's room. One figure kicked the door open and entered the room with a martial arts shout. Ellen, dressed only in an expensive nightgown and still wearing makeup, immediately turned on the light and sprung out of bed, shouting at the intruders. A security camera in her room recorded the entire encounter.

Facing the two warriors in close quarters in her room, she picked up a cane from the floor beside her bed. She swung it towards her attackers, which forced her assailant to miss; his blade came down with fierce energy on the mattress where she had just been sleeping, almost cleaving it in half.

Ellen struck her table lamp on her backswing as she flailed in her own defense. The light shade went flying towards the window and struck the closed shades. She swung back into position to counter the attack and snarled a fierce martial scream.

The Secret Service agent at the end of the second-story walkway heard the sound and fired a shot into the air to alert all. The two intruders had no choice but to withdraw hastily from the room. Ellen followed them, swinging wildly in their direction as they leaped from the second floor to the top of a van parked below, scrambled off, and then ran into the nearby woods. They shouted something unintelligible as they left the area. By this time, the Secret Service agents had taken up positions again in front of Ellen's room.

Newspaper reporters just happened to be staying in adjacent rooms on both sides of Ellen's. When it was clear that the situation was under control, they both came out to interview Ellen and the Secret Service agents. One of the agents allowed them to watch the security footage.

By the following morning, the story was all over the news. Someone had attempted to kill the presidential contender. The interview reporters surmised that Wild West Jenny was somehow behind the attempt.

***

The election was only two weeks away, and early voting had already started. The following day, Jenny was met by a covey of reporters who demanded to know whether she was responsible for the attempt on Ellen Winthrop's life. Major newspapers in Washington, New York, Chicago, and Los Angeles were already running stories about the incident.

Jenny called a press conference in the White House for later that morning. A room of frenzied reporters assembled to see what she had to say. She walked into the assembly and assumed her position behind a microphone mounted on the podium at the front of the room.

The first question was easy to answer. "Did you try to kill the other candidate?"

"No." Was her simple response.

"Did someone in your party attempt to kill her?"

"I hope not. I gave my subordinates strict instructions not to kill my opponent until after the election."

"You think this is a joke?" One of the reporters looked shocked.

"You think it's not?" Jenny smiled.

"Can you explain yourself?"

"Let's start with the latest election poll. I'm leading by a large margin. It's not that I've done anything complicated; I've just done my best to keep the government out of the way of the true economic heroes in our economy."

A burly reporter from one of the primary news services asked. "Are you suggesting that Ellen Winthrop set up a fake assassination attempt against herself to portray you in a bad light?"

"It is not my job to determine exactly what happened. In fact, there is virtually no time for anyone to undertake such an investigation before the election. But here is what I do know, Ellen is seriously losing. Americans don't want an economy where too many are engaged in rudimentary agriculture. Americans don't want the government to determine how much energy they or their businesses can use. Previous administrations have destroyed a lot of wealth. The elderly, in particular, faced hardships during the previous administration that were greater than anything they had confronted in the last hundred years. We can bring this country back together, but it will take much work. The last four years have been a good start, but we still have a long way to go. When it's my turn to leave office, I hope to leave the country in much better shape than it was when I took office. I wish Ellen well, but I don't wish any more of her leadership on our country."

The room was quiet. Jenny remained poised at the microphone, waiting for the next question. It was from a conservative news service, and Jenny recognized the reporter immediately.

"Can you confirm that former President Winthrop was behind all the food kitchen bombings during her last few days in office?"

"Can you think of anyone else that would have benefitted as much from making life miserable for the incoming President?"

Once again, the room was quiet. The reporters were frantically exchanging text messages with their newsrooms.

Jenny excused herself from the news conference and returned to the Oval Office. Her press secretary took the rest of the questions.

Rumor had it that Ellen Winthrop threw a severe tantrum at one of her rallies later that day. Her behavior was recorded by someone's cell phone and the event went viral.

Oddities
November 2040

Polls don't always reflect reality. The United States underwent a considerable transformation over the past four years. Jenny had terminated a large portion of the federal government's staff. Suffocating regulations had been disregarded, but so had protective ones. Many were leaving the country to move back to the cities. There was considerable dislocation and numerous homeless.

States and territories were responsible for managing the voting administration. Yet, in this new world, they were resource-challenged. While the general economy had recently improved, some states were doing better and some were not.

Jenny had been more worried about winning votes than managing the election process. She felt certain that she was in a stronger position than she had been four years earlier when she had been elected.

As it turned out, the devil was in the details.

Almost anyone who sought United States citizenship could quickly attain it. The application was short, and the approval was immediate. Almost no one even wasted time with a ceremony. For the government, it was a simple calculus. Citizens paid taxes and got little back in return.

There were no more illegal immigrants. Everyone had the right to enter the country, become a citizen, and vote. The law that formalized this arrangement had been in place for more than a decade.

Jenny did pay attention to the new voting software nationally implemented in every state. It allowed citizens to register and vote on whatever electronic devices they had access to. She had tested it herself and confirmed that it required voter identification. She was satisfied that it worked.

What Jenny had overlooked was another technical software application entitled "Solicitations for Proxy". It had been developed to allow stockholders to convey their voting rights to corporate management. It had recently been tweaked so that it could be used in conjunction with the new voting software.

Voters could sell their voting rights to a third party that was empowered to vote on their behalf. The amount of payment depended on the state where the voter was registered and when the vote was cast.

To get paid, eligible voters simply submitted their username and password for the voting software to the proxy application software and also provided their bank information. The proxy software featured an intuitive interface that made it easy to navigate, even for an elderly voter. Once the credentials were confirmed, funds were transmitted electronically, usually within twenty-four hours. Suffice it to say that this system revolutionized the way that voting was managed.

Proxy votes conveyed in tight swing states might be worth a hundred times more than proxy votes conveyed in races that weren't close. However, that was only true if the races were still close. Once a sufficient voting margin cushion was assured, the spot price for votes fell sharply. The proxy system generally encouraged voters to cast their votes early.

Jenny refused to contribute campaign funds to buy these votes. Ellen had no compunction in doing so and had billionaire friends overseas willing to support her cause.

So, when the final vote tally was counted, Jenny won the popular vote by a large margin. However, Ellen won the Electoral College vote by a slim margin.

Jenny was crushed. Many in the country were in shock. The good times were over.

Jenny could not fault people for selling their vote. If they didn't care who won, then what difference did it make who they allowed to cast their vote for them?

She was a bit rattled to discover that twice as many people had voted in swing states than were estimated to live there. However, with so many transient people moving around the country, many did not have a physical address. Her party had neither the time nor resources to run down the living situation for every voter.

It was easy to get citizenship in the United States and apparently just as easy to claim residence in any state. That feature corrupted the Electoral College system and led to this bizarre result.

It dawned on Jenny, that some voters may have been misled. The third party running the proxy service had not advertised who they were casting their votes for. Perhaps these voters had mistakenly assumed that the third party would vote to continue Jenny's programs.

Her "hands-off" management had done wonders for the economy. Still, everything her administration had accomplished was about to be reversed much sooner than most people in the country had hoped for or deserved. With tears in her eyes, she conceded the election on national television.

Moving Forward
January 2041

Jose was sure that his venture was dead in the water. He anticipated that his business economics could not withstand the challenge of operating without access to fossil fuels.

His investors agreed and directed him to sell his potted plants to a company in New Mexico. The other nursery sent a truck and picked up the plants and his advisers before inauguration day.

He and his sisters secured vegetable seeds for the next growing season.

***

After taking their company public during the latter part of the previous fall, Rose, Johnse, Linda, and Clare placed their restricted stock with a Brazilian company. That corporation had operations throughout South America, where it hoped to capitalize on their brand awareness.

Paul joined them, and the five of them traveled to Sao Paulo where they were promised employment as set out in their agreement. Clare was in her second trimester and comfortable with traveling.

They immediately fell in love with the country and Clare, Johnse, and Rose started to learn Portuguese. They all shared a small apartment not far from Parque Ibirapuera, a large park that partly surrounded a lake, where they often took long walks with their baby stroller. Their corporate office was on Paulista Avenue, a very attractive commercial district.

Rose thought their first mission would be to explore ways to produce their ethanol from sugar cane, a less expensive approach than the recipe they had used in Pikeville.

285

Johnse's brother, Billy, had recently passed, essentially from alcohol poisoning. He never learned to go lightly on the tasty, but potent, ethanol they peddled. While he died with a smile on his face, it was a sobering reminder of their product's dark side.

***

Eacher and Irene returned to his farm in Arkansas. The neighbor had set aside some of the previous year's harvest for them; it looked like they would have plenty of stored vegetables until the start of the next growing season. Since they were not interested in farming themselves, they hoped that they could extend their deal with their neighbor.

Jasmine's job in Atlanta disappeared, and she joined them in Arkansas.

***

Jenny left town before the inauguration. It wasn't clear where she had gone, but she left Tex to handle all her administration's transition details. He returned to his ranch and handed the details with a conference call in the morning. Between the two, they electronically signed many pardons to protect those who they had encouraged to skirt the laws and regulations.

The businesses that had bet on her re-election were scaling back. Most were curtailing their operations and laying staff off. Others were taking action to get their foreign workers out of the country before oppressive carbon taxes got reinstated.

***

Ellen's political calculations had paid off, but she didn't want to think about all the money that her supporters had contributed on her behalf. It was a huge "I owe you" that they would collect in various ways over the next four years. Any previous supporters that had deserted her, like Mike, would find that their assets in the United States would now be subject to close examination.

She imagined a future where the government determined how and where people lived and dictated what energy they would be permitted to expend. Ellen was back in her element.

She had never believed the planet was at risk of overheating from manmade carbon dioxide emissions. There had been plenty of opportunity for those scary predictions to come true, and they hadn't. Most likely, the forces that now controlled the weather had controlled it for many millions of years. The suggestion that humanity was so essential that it now controlled the climate was superstitious, hubristic, and absurd.

Nevertheless, persistent claims by academics, activists, and the media never faltered and it was not in her party's interest to change their tune.

Incidentally, certain states threatened to secede. Her government needed to address that issue quickly after she took office. She strongly preferred to simply permit them to leave the Union without a fight; her government did not have the will or resources to compel them to stay.

Still, she needed to canvas her financial supporters. In her mind, it was a contractual issue, not a patriotic one.

***

Marco strode confidently to the podium microphone and adjusted it lower. He was wearing a crisp blue wool suit and a yellow tie. His shoes were patent leather and gleamed brightly in the light. Newly elected from Houston, he addressed the Texas State House of Representatives. "Too long have we allowed ourselves to be held captive by a political party that ignores our best interests; I spit on their claim to this state and willingly put my life at risk to break the ties that hold us together." He stopped to gaze at others seated around the assembly.

"Yes, many of you are from that other party, but we are brothers and sisters today. We rise against a defective national government that wants to place our strong state into shackles and our workers in chains. There is no going back. Not now. Not ever."

The assembly bristled from the courage and determination in his voice. There might be a fight or not, but there would be a divorce. The national government had no right to implement another economic contraction. Texas will go its own way, and the only question in his mind was who else would join them. He returned to his seat amid the applause of his peers.

General Comments

I'm unable to imagine how our country could transition from our current economic situation to one where we quickly and almost completely eliminate fossil fuels.

For starters, we'd all need to be absolutely convinced that more manmade emissions would have devastating consequences for the world's climate in the future. Our fears would need to be so compelling that we'd all willingly give up our living standards.

Such a belief would need to persist for many years.

We'd need the stomach and commitment to press on as our electrical grid fell apart before our eyes. Surely that would be a serious indicator that would make many reconsider the project.

Our country would bankrupt itself persisting in this scheme. China is ahead in wind turbines, solar panels, and battery technology – so there's a good chance we'd run up some serious national debts buying such products from them.

Our politicians would need to outlaw climate science criticism and those decisions would need to be widely supported. It's easier to imagine political intolerance than to believe that the enhanced carbon dioxide hypothesis could be sufficiently credible to withstand even a modest amount of scrutiny.

Both political parties smoked the same dope and were selling us on the need for our collective commitment to decarbonize.

We all lost our concerns for bird and bat deaths from wind turbines and were fine with industrializing our landscapes.

Finally, China and India would have to stop building additional coal and natural gas power plants. They'd also have to be willing to start aggressively reducing their national carbon dioxide emissions on the same timeline as the other countries focused on decarbonization. The bottom line is that global manmade carbon dioxide emissions will continue to increase until they do so. In short, trying to understand why we would implement Net Zero policy would require a lot of assurances and some basic common sense. All of this seems very improbable to me.

Perhaps it would have been more credible had I inserted a Fairy Godmother who waved her wand and eliminated fossil fuels from our society. She could also magically create vast numbers of utility-scale batteries (without concern for the incredible costs involved!), install all the system management necessary (like spinning support for Reactive Power etc.), build vast long-distance transmission lines to deliver electricity to our major population centers, grid interconnections to share power between electrical regions, overcome high costs of capital, and pacify local community resistance to nearby wind turbines.

The point is that reality is considerably more stubborn than this simple story suggests. Let's hope that the democratic system is equally robust to withstand this assault on our common sense.

Of course, if a Fairy Godmother could really wave her magic wand and transition our energy system, why not forget about wind turbines and solar panels all together. Why not ask her to build us a nuclear-powered energy system?

With that approach, we could replace fossil fuels, except perhaps for the ongoing need for synthetic fertilizer and petrochemicals, and provide the nation with virtually unlimited, reliable and dispatchable energy. We could even overbuild our existing electrical capacity that would allow us to support all the upcoming demand for data centers and other technology-related demands on our infrastructure. Heck, with nuclear power, we could even throw in a hydrogen infrastructure and imagine fuel-celled vehicles and electrical vehicles as the dominant modes of transportation.

Even if a Fairy Godmother could magically make all the changes for our infrastructure, we'd be foolish to insist that it would be one driven by wind and solar electrical generation. Think of the difficulty of replacing all that hardware within the next twenty years and again every twenty years after that. Imagine all the trash and hazardous waste that would have to be dealt with.

290

Nuclear energy is our "go to" energy source for the next few thousand years for mankind. It's got a much smaller footprint and will be augmented by fusion energy at some point.

It would be a much different story if I had described such a transition. Since we're not already doing it confirms that we're not really serious about decarbonization or even an energy transition.

***

Here's a graph to keep in mind that I previously showcased in Poorly Zeroed.

Here's a drawing from 1956 by Marion King Hubbert.

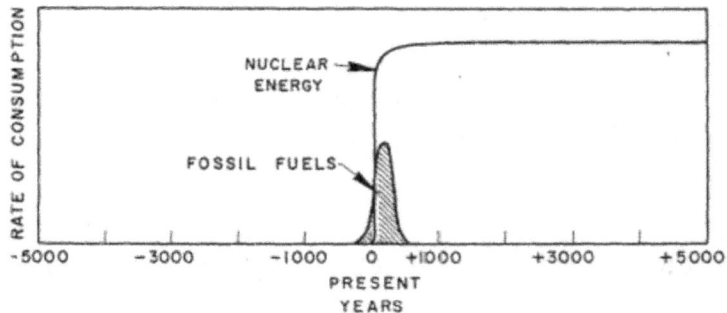

Relative magnitudes of possible fossil-fuel and nuclear-energy consumption seen in time perspective of +/- 5,000 years. [1]

---

[1] Figure from Hubbert's 1956 paper, *Nuclear Energy and the Fossil Fuels*, https://mkinghubbert.wordpress.com/2009/03/08/hubberts-early-take-on-nuclear-energy/

References

The Center for Environmental Research and Earth Sciences (CERES). "**The urban heat island: implications for global warming & climate change**". Ceres-Science. 2024. https://www.youtube.com/watch?v=8Q9vj1F4Xkg&t=4s

Clintel. **The Frozen Climate Views of the IPCC: An Analysis of AR6**. Clintel Foundation. 2023.
Curry, Judith. Climate Uncertainty and Risk: Rethinking our Response. Anthem Press. 2023.

Dilley, David. "**Global Warming Will be Dead by 2030**". Tom Nelson Podcasts #216. Youtube. 2024. https://www.youtube.com/watch?v=NeFePI1nW1Y&t=2s

Durkin, Martin. **Climate: The Movie (The Cold Truth)**. United Kingdom. 2023. Climate: The Movie (The Cold Truth) Updated 4K version (youtube.com). https://www.youtube.com/watch?v=zmfRG8-RHEI

Koonin, Steven. "**Steven Koonin on The Limitations of Climate Change Models.**" Hoover Institution. https://www.youtube.com/watch?v=acyErLNL7kQ . 2023.

Lindzen, Richard et al. "**Fossil Fuels and Greenhouse Gases (GHGs) Climate Science.**" Lindzen-Happer-Koonin-climate-science-4-24.pdf (co2coalition.org). 2024.

May, Andy. **Politics & Climate Change: A History.** American Freedom Publications LLC. 2020.
292

Poyet, Patrice. **The Rational Climate e-Book: Cooler is Riskier** (the Extended 2nd Edition). ResearchGate.net. 2022. https://www.researchgate.net/publication/347150306_The_Rational_Climate_e-Book_2nd_Edition (*free e-book*).

Vinós, Javier. **Solving the Climate Puzzle: The Sun's Surprising Role**. Critical Science Press. 2023.

Acknowledgments

Many thanks to my reviewers and their insights. Mary Cozine, Lou Pelz, Rob Krotee, Joe Barber, Bob Forbes, Phillip Hotchkiss, Jim Kelly and Linda Williams.

I also acknowledge the insights and perseverance from all those leaders on the nonfiction side of Net Zero and Climate Science. A few of them are listed in the References section with some of their most recent publications and studies.

Some of my other favorites include Jim Steel (the ecologist), John Robson with the "Climate Discussion Nexus", Anthony Watt with "Watt's Up with That", and Patrick Moore. A number of these later sources, and others, were listed in the references for **Poorly Zeroed**.

I also regularly read the materials from the Global Warming Policy Foundation as well as those from the Net Zero Watch.

About the Author

John graduated from the Stanford Graduate School of Business, the United States Military Academy at West Point, and the US Army Ranger School. A licensed professional engineer and long-term energy consultant, he self-published **Poorly Zeroed** in 2022 and previously co-authored **Oil Dusk**. He served as an engineer with the US Army Corps of Engineers in Saudi Arabia, commanded an engineering company, and taught economics to West Point cadets.

Books by This Author

Poorly Zeroed: A Net Zero Travesty
By John M. Cape

Seeking to decarbonize rapidly, the United States rushed to
abandon fossil fuels with predictable consequences. In the
near future, energy is scarce, and the economy has been
decimated. China is now the world's only superpower. Aged
climate skeptics confirm that the climate science used to
justify Net Zero was a deliberate overreach. They risk their
lives to share their insights.

Oil Dusk: A Peak Oil Story
By John M. Cape and Laura Buckner

The MacCasland family struggles to survive when the dollar
crashes and the United States is starved for oil. Gas prices
soar, store shelves empty and jobs are almost nonexistent.
When brutal gangs start looting, it becomes clear that anyone
still living in the suburbs needs a Plan B.